William John Loftie

Memorials of the Savoy

the palace - the hospital - the chapel

William John Loftie

Memorials of the Savoy
the palace - the hospital - the chapel

ISBN/EAN: 9783337094386

Printed in Europe, USA, Canada, Australia, Japan

Cover: Foto ©Andreas Hilbeck / pixelio.de

More available books at **www.hansebooks.com**

MEMORIALS OF THE

SAVOY

The Palace: The Hospital: The Chapel

By The Rev. WILLIAM JOHN LOFTIE, B.A., F.S.A.

ASSISTANT CHAPLAIN OF THE SAVOY

AUTHOR OF 'IN AND OUT OF LONDON,' 'THE LATIN YEAR,' ETC.

WITH AN APPENDIX OF ORIGINAL DOCUMENTS

CONTRIBUTED BY CHARLES TRICE MARTIN, B.A., F.S.A.

OF THE PUBLIC RECORD OFFICE

And a Preface

By The Rev. HENRY WHITE, M.A.

CHAPLAIN OF THE SAVOY, AND CHAPLAIN IN ORDINARY TO THE QUEEN

London

MACMILLAN AND CO.

1878

Dedication.

THESE MEMORIALS OF THE

ROYAL PALACE AND CHAPEL OF THE SAVOY

ARE DEDICATED,

BY SPECIAL PERMISSION,

TO

HER MOST GRACIOUS MAJESTY

QUEEN VICTORIA.

PREFACE.

IN the year 1844 Mr. Gibson Lockhart, the son-in-law
and biographer of Sir Walter Scott, was commanded to
write "An Account of the Royal Chapel of the Savoy."
His short pamphlet was printed at the cost of Her Most
Gracious Majesty the Queen, and was destined only for
private circulation.

No other attempt has ever been made to present a
monograph on the Savoy. The following pages are
devoted to an ample and accurate record of the varied
attractions and associations which cluster around the
history of this ancient precinct.

I do not crave any apology for going in quest of a
wide and sympathetic welcome for this Volume. The
eager and endless inquiries for such a book abundantly
vindicate the present venture.

As I have not wrought anything towards an accomplishment of the design which these Memorials achieve, I may avow, with beseeming grace, that the intention has been most effectively fulfilled. My colleague has bestowed the choicest gifts of his well-known skill and care to present the most exact and interesting information within his grasp. In unaffected confidence I commit this book to the acceptance and approval of any who may be pleased to read it.

I cannot close this Preface until I have offered my humble and grateful acknowledgments of the condescension of the Queen in allowing us to dedicate these Memorials to Her Most Gracious Majesty. I must add my very fervent thanks to the Author; to the Committee of the Society for Promoting Christian Knowledge for leave to reprint a chapter from *In and Out of London*, written for the Society by the Rev. William Loftie; to Mr. Charles Trice Martin for the valuable Collections from the Rolls Office, some of which find place in the Appendix; and to Mr. James Foster Wadmore for leave to make an etching from a valuable picture by J. M. W. Turner, R.A. A tribute of gratitude is also due to other some, both of friends and strangers, who, in lesser degree, have contributed to augment the success of this endeavour.

The Author bids me to add that the notices of eminent men only pretend to trace their connection with the Savoy. Complete biographies of such worthies as the Archbishop of Spalato, Archbishop Sheldon, Bishop Douglas, and Dr. Thomas Fuller, would claim more space than could be spared within the compass of this small Volume.

For myself, I own that the issue of this book sets one of the happiest marks upon the long and cherished intimacy which I have enjoyed with all that has concerned the Chapel and Precinct of the Savoy during the past eighteen years.

HENRY WHITE.

All Saints' Day, 1878.

MEMORIALS OF THE SAVOY.

CHAPTER I.

The Origin of the Savoy.

A time when there was no such place—The ancient limits of Westminster—The Strand six centuries ago—Foreshore—Peter of Savoy—A cargo of ladies—Lake Leman—The Savoy boundaries.

THOUGH we have all heard of a time

"When Britain first at Heaven's command,
Arose from out the azure main;"

it would puzzle us to assign the exact date. Yet we must in our opening chapter endeavour to find the date at which that piece of Britain in which we Savoyards are most interested, was rescued from the Thames—when, in fact, the Savoy, instead of arising from out the azure main, saw the azure main, if the muddy water of the river can even poetically be

The origin of the Savoy.

called azure, retreat from the Strand, and leave behind the strip of firm ground on which we stand.

A time when there was no such place.

The first thing I have to do, then, is to go back until I find a time when there was certainly no Savoy, and afterwards to feel my way down the stream of years until I see it gradually emerge into the daylight. Fortunately we have documentary evidence from which to make our very first start.

The ancient limits of Westminster.

In the year 951 King Edgar defined the limits of Westminster in a charter which he granted to the Abbey. From it we learn, by inference, that no such place as the Savoy existed, nay more, that Fleet Street and the Strand, and all that now lies between them and the river, had not yet emerged. The southern boundary of the parish and manor was the river; St. Clement Danes is not mentioned, neither is the Temple, St. Mary-le-Strand, Charing Cross, nor Whitehall. In fact, we may very safely gather from the charter that there were no houses, probably no dry land, between the high ground on which Lincoln's Inn and Covent Garden now stand and the water's edge. Indeed we may go farther. Contrary to what you will find in most histories of London, I think it will be safe to conclude that there was no street or road leading to

Ludgate along what we call the Strand and Fleet Street; that, in fact, Ludgate, as its name imports (Fludgate or Floodgate), was an exit from the City by water. This charter of 951 gives us " London Fen " as the eastern boundary of Westminster, and we must picture to ourselves a wide marsh extending from very near Temple Bar to Ludgate, and from near the Holborn Viaduct to the foot of Blackfriars Bridge. Through the marsh a tidal river, the Fleet, made its way, just as the Lea makes its way still through green meadows to the Thames, and barges are moored here and there under the City wall to receive passengers and merchandise.

We may thus see that nine hundred and twenty-five years ago there was no such place as the Savoy.

The next piece of information of a documentary kind is a decree made in 1222 for terminating a dispute between the Bishop of London and the Abbot of Westminster. In this decree the boundaries are once more given, but they no longer extend on the east to the " London Fen," for the parish of St. Giles's is excepted, and a line is drawn from the house of one " Simon, the weaver," which must have been in or near what we know as Drury Lane, to the Innocents' Church, which stood very near the present gate of King's College, and from thence to the

The origin of the Savoy.

"Ulebrig," which, under the name of Ivy Bridge, crossed a little brook near the present Cecil Street, and so along the highway to Westminster.

The existence of the church, the bridge, and the highway, show us, first, that there was dry land on the south side of the Strand, and secondly, that though that dry land had not yet received a name, it was excepted from the Abbey Manor and parish of St. Margaret's.

Foreshore.

We have thus seen that by degrees a piece of land was reclaimed from the Thames between the City and Westminster, and remarked that in 1222 it was still nameless. We next observe that this piece of land belonged to the King; and if we inquire how the King obtained it, seeing it was bounded on the one side by the property of Westminster Abbey, and on the other by the Thames, we must remember that even at the present day the Queen of England is entitled to "fore-shore," that is, to land left dry at low tide, and that the fact of the King owning our piece of ground goes to confirm the inferential history I have given of it above.

In 1236 Henry III. married Eleanor of Provence, and within a very few years we find the Queen's poor relations crowding into England to see what they could obtain. One of her uncles was made Archbishop of Canterbury, and to another was given a vast and fair estate in Yorkshire. But a town house was needful for a residence, when the royal nephew and niece should be at their palace at Westminster; and in 1246, on the 12th February, a date which we may look upon as our name day, if not our birthday, a grant of the land lying between the Thames and the street called "la Straunde," was made by King Henry to his "beloved uncle," Peter of Savoy.

The origin of the Savoy.

Let us pause for a moment to inquire as to the state of this part of London when Count Peter took possession of the manor which was henceforth to be known by his name.

Peter of Savoy.

Six hundred years ago the way from London to Westminster was not as it is now, through noisy and crowded streets, but over the silent waters of the Thames. A road existed by which, it is true, the land passage might be made. It skirted the shore of the river, but at some distance, and kept high on the side of the hill from the Temple Bar to Charing Cross. How much of it was really a road, and how much was a mere track, it would now be impossible to say. At the village of Charing it turned to the south, still keeping parallel with the shore, and entered the royal precincts, for though Whitehall and St. James's were still

The origin of the Savoy.

unbuilt, the park, open to palace and the abbey, extended from the king's mews southward to Westminster, and westward to the Mall. The abbot's garden and Spring Gardens were not divided except by roads and pathways from the fields now marked by Long Acre, or the more distant country on the ridge of the hill by St. Giles's Church in the outskirts of Holborn. Many of the names which still serve to identify these sites, such as the lane of St. Martin, and the church dedicated to him "in the fields," are of modern origin; but a succession of gardens and pleasure-grounds covered all the slope from the city boundary at the Earl of Lincoln's House, near St. Dunstan's and St. Clement's, to the gardens of the king's palace, which formed the northern and eastern approach to Westminster. There were a few more houses congregated at Charing and St. Clement's than at other points on the route. But all the land which lay to south of the highway, and between it and the river's edge, belonged to the great manor of which the town house of Peter of Savoy, the queen's uncle, formed the centre. Much of this strip of coast was then or within a few years occupied by the villas of great nobles, and their names survive in the little streets which now occupy their place. At the time when Count Peter made his residence among them, however, the situation was too insecure to tempt many who could not, like the religious houses, or the bishops, defy, with the terrors of the supernatural, predatory bands and riotous soldiery. As the event proved, this caution was not unfounded.

Whether the count made here a residence worthy of his almost regal state, or only used the site for a modest lodge or manor house, we have no means of determining. From the way in which his name was henceforth linked to the place, it seems unlikely that his building was of a merely temporary kind. It is quite possible, and even probable, that he built a well-defended and secure residence, if not a fortified and moated mansion, such as those which all over England still attest at once the magnificence and the insecurity of the nobles of the thirteenth century.

The family of the Count of Savoy occupied in those days a place not unlike that now filled in Europe by some of the princely houses of Germany. It was ancient and noble, if not yet illustrious, and by a hereditary custom its younger scions sought their fortunes in love, war, or religion, anywhere but at home. They formed brilliant alliances; they fought in well-contested battles; they attained high dignity in the Church. The little county of Savoy, with various claims, more or less substantial, on the possessions of their neighbours, and a standing quarrel with the citizens of Geneva, formed the moderate patrimony of the head of the house. But ages of activity, of talent, and of necessity, have resulted in the development of the last count and duke of Savoy into a king of Sardinia, and of the last king of Sardinia, by the sacrifice of the paternal principality, into the monarch of a united Italy.

Born in 1203 at Susa, Peter, the seventh son of Thomas, Count of Savoy, was himself for a time in holy orders, and was the brother of two archbishops, and the uncle of five queens. We are not concerned with his foreign career. His influence on English history commences with his coming to England. He probably had heard from others of the rich prizes to be gained in the kingdom of his niece's husband, and may have needed no special invitation to prove its hospitality. He was poor, he was brave, he was clever. These were sufficient reasons for his coming, and they will perhaps account for his stay, varied by occasional excursions to the Continent, for the long period of twenty-three years. The "Second Charlemagne," as he was surnamed by some, landed at Dover on the 5th January 1241, and was met by the king himself with every demonstration of joy and family affection. He was immediately invested with the honour of Richmond, once the princely estate of the Dukes of Brittany, to whom the earldom may be supposed to have still belonged, as it was never held as a title by Count Peter. Matthew Paris and his double of Westminster, if indeed there were two distinct chroniclers of the name, call him more than once Earl of Richmond; but in formal documents he is described always as Peter of Savoy, or in the Latin of the day, " de Sabaudia," with the usual addition of the words, " Avunculus Domini Regis," the uncle of our Lord the King. The Duke of Brittany, indeed, on one occasion, as appears by a letter still extant,* interfered on behalf of his old tenants in Yorkshire, and remonstrated with Peter for the tyrannical exactions with which he oppressed the monks of Jervaulx, and exercised his territorial rights.

Two months after his arrival in England, namely, on the 18th of March, being St. Edward's day, he was knighted by Henry. It would be tedious, and quite apart from our present purpose, to follow and trace out all the notices of his movements which occur among

---

* *Shirley*, vol. ii. Shirley dates this letter in 1262. There are reasons for believing this is at least ten years too late.

the records. He went several times to France
on diplomatic missions, was arbiter to determine various delicate questions respecting Simon
de Montfort, Aymer de Valence, and Edward,
the King's eldest son. In February 1246 he
was in England, and in 1247 he was on his way
back from a residence of some months in France,
but both these dates require to be noticed rather
more at length.

The first, Feb. 12, 1246, is the date of the
grant to him by Henry III. of the manor now
so long called after him. The King was at
Reading when he signed it. The annual rent
to be paid was mentioned as *three barbed
arrows* at Michaelmas. The lands were defined as those which had belonged to Brian de
L'Isle, "outside the walls of our city of
London, in the street called the Strand" (*extra
muros civitatis nostræ Londiniæ, in vico qui
vocatur La Straunde*). This grant probably
only comprised the ground on which the house
itself stood, and we find two additions made to
its extent during the occupation of Peter. One,
which was obtained from the sisters of the hospital of St. James, was of lands "opposite the
church of the Innocents, towards the south,"
over which they had a claim of sixteen-pence
rent. The other on the west, which he obtained from Bartholomew de Venyt, comprised

the ground remaining between that which had belonged to Brian "de Insula," and that held by the Bishop of Carlisle.

The boundaries of the estate were afterwards defined, and to understand them now we must remember that west of Wych Street, then or soon afterwards known as the Old Wych Road, or Aldwych Road, there was an open green with a Maypole, and just beyond it a cemetery, which lay rather below the level of the present line of the street, and on a part of site now occupied by Somerset House. A chapel which adjoined the burial-place was perhaps rather nearer the river ; this was the Innocents', mentioned above, but it afterwards became the church of St. Mary le Strand, and was destroyed by the Protector Somerset to make way for his palace. Still farther to the west, almost exactly opposite to where Catherine Street now enters the Strand, was the Strand Cross, and opposite to it the house and garden of the Bishop of Coventry. All these sites were far below the present level, and the slope must have been very steep to the edge of the river. A little bit of very modest engineering here foreshadowed the Holborn Viaduct and such great works of our own day. At the point now marked by the approach to Waterloo Bridge, a steep lane descended to the water's side, the

The origin of the Savoy.
roadway of the Strand crossing over it by a bridge. This lane formed the eastern boundary of the house of Peter of Savoy. Three sides of the plat of ground are thus made clear, the northern, along which ran "La Strand," the southern, which was formed by the Thames, and the eastern, which we have seen to be conterminous with the Strand Lane. The fourth side was bounded by the house and garden of the Bishop of Carlisle, which stood where Beaufort Buildings stand now.

What use Peter made of his land we cannot tell, nor what kind of house he built upon the site. We do not find any accounts of money laid out for him by the King, and it is not very likely he had much of his own to spend. Still something must have been built, and that it was of some importance may be inferred, first, because of the way in which his name has been connected with the place ever since, and secondly, because of some expressions relating to the buildings in a document to which we shall have occasion to refer in the next chapter.

A cargo of Ladies.
The residence in England of Peter of Savoy was varied, as we have already seen, by several excursions to the Continent, and one of these took place very soon after the grant of this land. On his return he brought with him a cargo which seems to have added greatly to the un-

popularity already incurred in England by the foreign relatives of King Henry and Queen Eleanor. He was accompanied, we read, by a party of young ladies from the foreign courts where he had visited, with the open intention of marrying them to the wards of his nephew. The King's wards in those days included all the young nobles of the greatest estates, and all such children as would now be called Wards of Chancery ; and this singular importation, strange and distasteful as it seems to our ideas, was even more so to the English of that day, whose insular prejudices were increased and fostered by the difficulty of travelling and the ignorance of foreign countries. The undertaking of Peter was, however, so far successful that several young gentlemen of high rank, including, according to some accounts, Richard de Burgh, were captivated by the charming foreigners, and in April and May 1247, marriages, under the Queen's personal care, and to the great disgust of the natives, took place, as Matthew says, " *molestum et absurdum.*" The hatred of the foreigners was thus largely increased, and was still more highly inflamed by the conduct of Archbishop Boniface of Savoy, Peter's brother.

The weakness of King John and his political exigencies had placed the kingdom in the power of the Pope, especially in ecclesiastical

The origin of the Savoy.

matters. The legal forms by which the English Church was newly bound were particularly disliked, and the large influx of foreign clergymen was a constant cause of irritation. We cannot here enter on any of the questions by which the popular mind was agitated. Lyons, the archbishopric of one of Peter's brothers, was at that time the place of residence of the Papal Court, and thither the champion of the liberties of the English Church, Robert Grosseteste twice journeyed, in order, if possible, to counteract the disastrous measures by which the religious life of his countrymen was impeded and oppressed. On his return from the second of these pilgrimages he died, and there were not wanting among the people those who looked upon him as a martyr. Matthew Paris mentions that the value of benefices then held by foreigners in England was calculated to be above the whole sum of the King's revenue. The church was impoverished by the rapacity of non-resident prelates, some of whom had never visited their sees, while others had only come over to increase and levy their exactions. Grosseteste addresses many remonstrances to these men, and frequently refers to their doings in a tone almost of despair. There was no greater transgressor among them than the brother of Peter de Savoy, Boniface, Archbishop of Canterbury, who, though primate of the English Church, did not set foot in England for nine years after his appointment; when he did come it was to extort money. He took up his residence in London at the house of his nominee, the Bishop of Chichester, and by pretences of visitation endeavoured to obtain the same sums he had already obtained at Canterbury. A curious account of one of these attempts occurs incidentally in the *London Chronicles.** The canons of St. Bartholomew's successfully resisted the Archbishop, defeating him eventually on a point of law arising out of the wording of the City Charter. Boniface retired from England before the storm broke, which it did soon after the death of Grosseteste, the Queen's relations being expelled in 1257, as well as the King's half-brothers, William and Aymer de Valence. Peter seems to have avoided banishment by being abroad at the time of the council at Oxford, for in March 1250 and in 1255, letters are addressed to him respecting the truces with France and other business matters in which he was engaged on behalf of his nephew, King Henry. In the meantime he had been prosecuting the hereditary designs of his house upon Geneva. D'Aubigny † gives some account of

* Ryley, p. 18.
† *History of the Reformation in time of Calvin*, vol. i. 20.

The origin of the Savoy. his proceedings, but apparently supposed that they took place after he had been some time in England. If the date he gives, 1250, be correct, Peter can only have paid a flying visit to Geneva at the time he seized the castle, and had not yet been long enough in England "to study the art of Government." In a few years he seems to be permanently residing in England, and so continues, apparently for several years before 1259, when he is again abroad, and signs a letter, as witness, as to the exile of Aymer de Valence. In 1263 his nephew, Boniface, Count of Savoy, died, and Peter succeeded to the paternal domains. A year later, in 1264, we find Gilbert de Clare, Earl of Gloucester, appointed custodian of all his lands and possessions in England, and he does not seem ever to have returned. He spent the remaining years of his life in renewing his old quarrels at Geneva, but acknowledged himself beaten at last in 1267, when, as D'Aubigny says, he found himself weakened by age and exhausted by ceaseless activity. He retired to the Castle of Chillon, where, sailing every day

Lake Leman. on that beautiful lake, and listening to the music of a minstrel, he passed the last year of his life in luxurious ease, and died in 1268, leaving "The Savoy" to the friars of Mountjoy, who were confirmed in the posses-

sion of it by King Henry. They did not hold
it long, but in 1270 (10th April) sold it to
Queen Eleanor for 300 marks, a sum which
may be roughly calculated at about £3000 of
our money.

CHAPTER II.

𝕿𝖍𝖊 𝕮𝖆𝖗𝖑𝖘 𝖔𝖋 𝕷𝖆𝖓𝖈𝖆𝖘𝖙𝖊𝖗.

Edmund Crouchback — Queen Blanche — The Manor House repaired and fortified — The Gardens — The Red Rose — " Saint " Thomas of Lancaster — Henry, Earl of Lancaster.

Edmund Crouchback.

Two days before Queen Eleanor bought the Savoy, her second son, Edmund, who was now five and twenty years of age, was married in his father's magnificent new building, the Abbey Church of Westminster, to the Lady Aveline, the second, but now sole surviving, daughter of William de Fortibus, Earl of Albemarle.* She was the greatest heiress of her time, and was perhaps about eighteen when the wedding took place. Very soon after, the bridegroom and his elder brother, Prince Edward, set off for the

* There is much discrepancy among the authorities as to the date of this marriage. Dean Stanley places it in 1269.

Crusades. Aveline did not follow the heroic example set by the wife of the elder prince, but remained at home, and never saw her husband again. She died in 1273, and was buried in Westminster Abbey, close to the altar at which so short a time before she had stood as a bride. Her tomb, one of the earliest, as well as one of the most beautiful in the church, is familiar to all visitors, situated as it is, just within the rails of the sanctuary in the choir. Twenty-three years later her husband's body was brought home from Bayonne to rest in the same place.

Edmund of Lancaster has usually gone in history by the surname of *Crouchback*. There are reasons for believing that this name was given on account of the cross, or *crux*, assumed by him when he departed for Palestine. But, long after his death, a story was spread abroad by the partisans of the house of Lancaster that he had been deformed, and that the name *Crouchback* referred to the peculiar character of his deformity. The object of this assertion was evident. The Lancastrians were anxious to have it believed that being crooked, Prince *

---

* The term "prince," here and elsewhere applied to Edmund of Lancaster, is used for convenience only. In the thirteenth century and afterwards, a king's son would have been styled in English "the Lord Edmund," not "the Prince Edmund."

The Earls of Lancaster.

Edmund was put aside by his parents in favour of the brother, whose surname of *Longshanks* sufficiently indicates the superiority of his stature, if any such evidence were wanting at the present day. But as Prince Edward was more than five years of age when Edmund was born, namely, in January 1245, and as a daughter, the Lady Margaret, intervened between the brothers, the legend does not require any serious refutation.

In 1253 Prince Edmund was made Earl of Chester. In 1254 the Pope gave him the empty title of King of Sicily. Both these honours were afterwards taken from him. His cousin, Simon de Montfort, was made Earl of Chester in his stead in 1264, under colour of an exchange for the Earldom of Leicester, by which title Simon is best known, and the honour of Chester, in 1301, was conferred upon Prince Edward, and has ever since remained with the heirs-apparent to the crown of England. Edmund was made Earl of Leicester in 1264, and obtained ten years later a confirmation from his brother; and in 1267, on the 30th June, he was created Earl of Lancaster. The charter does not call him "Earl." It only grants him the honour, county, castle, and town of Lancaster. But the earldom was probably conferred by actual personal investiture with the sword *(per cincturam gladii)* ; and he was afterwards summoned to Parliament by the full title of Earl of Lancaster and Leicester, and Steward of England. But the Pope's gift of Sicily and Apulia was an honour of a different kind from either of the English earldoms. It meant that he must fight for his kingdom, and, considering that he was only nine years of age when he received the ring of investiture, we need not be surprised to find that a long time elapsed before he thought of a serious prosecution of his claim. His father, however, Henry III., saw in the Pope's present an admirable excuse for extorting money from his subjects; though, like so many of the same monarch's projects, the war for the conquest of Naples never became more than a project; and, in 1263, the Pope's empty grant was revoked.

It seems to have been on his way home from Palestine, after the death of his father and of his wife, that Earl Edmund wooed and won the hand of the lovely Queen of Navarre, Blanche, widow of Henri V., the grand-daughter of a king of France, and in every respect an eligible wife for the English prince. Their marriage took place in 1275, and the bride and bridegroom remained in Provence till the following year, when they came over to London, the Earl being anxious, as we are told in the quaint

The Earls of Lancaster.

Queen Blanche.

The Earls of Lancaster.

words of one of the monastic chroniclers,* to show his wife the pleasantness (*jocunditatem*) of his native land, namely, the kingdom of England, and the possessions he had in that kingdom. The Earl of Lancaster and the Queen of Navarre entered London in state, and were received with great joy, and magnificent demonstrations of welcome. The people had long forgotten that Edmund, through his unfortunate and absurd claim on Sicily, had been the innocent cause of the long civil wars between Henry III. and Simon de Montfort; and the beauty of Queen Blanche, his consort, was, no doubt, an assistance to his popularity. He was summoned to Parliament in December, and constantly took part in public affairs; but our interest is with what can hardly be called a matter of public concern, his first connection with the Savoy.

The manor-house repaired.

During the time it belonged to Queen Eleanor, we may believe that the manorial residence had been put into good repair and well furnished, while the grounds about it had been laid out and formed into gardens, and pleasure-grounds, such as surrounded all the other noble mansions along the Strand. That the Queen's improvements cannot have been very great we shall presently have occasion to

* *Ann. Monast.*, vol. iv., p. 269. Rolls Series.

infer. But we may suppose with reason that the Savoy was surrounded with gardens and orchards, and that the fruits and flowers already known in England were to be found there, as well as in the gardens of the Earl of Lincoln, or those of the Abbot of Westminster close by. Matthew Paris complains in the year 1257 of the scarcity of figs, cherries, plums, and nuts of all kinds, as if such things had previously been quite common. That the Queen's house was in good repair may be drawn from the fact that when, in 1265, Prince Edward, brought home his young and devoted wife, Eleanor of Castile, she was lodged in the Savoy, and thenceforth made it her town residence whenever she came to London. In 1279 it was assigned for the lodging of the King of Scotland, who came to attend a parliament. This was Alexander III., the King's brother-in-law, the extinction of whose line, by the death on her way from Norway of his grand-daughter and successor, Margaret, was the occasion of the fierce war which King Edward carried on at the close of his long reign. The French Chronicle of London* says he was lodged between the "courts" of the Bishop of Chichester and the Earl of Lancaster (in the place) called the "Saveye." This may mean that Edmund of Lancaster was already in the

* *Camden Society*, 1844, p. 15.

Savoy, and that a temporary residence for King Alexander was made between the two houses of the Earl and the Bishop, and on the intervening ground ; or else that the Earl had a residence at one side of the Savoy, which then, as we have seen, belonged to the dowager Queen, Eleanor of Provence. It is quite possible that Earl Edmund, with his wife Queen Blanche, resided in his mother's house, especially as the old queen does not seem to have herself made much use of it. But, be this as it may, in 1284 we find him in full possession.

After the death of Henry III., Queen Eleanor, his widow, had as it were gravitated to the cloister. She did not actually take the veil till 1286, but two years earlier she was residing in the neighbourhood of Amesbury, where she subsequently professed herself a nun ; and it is at the royal Castle of Ludgershall, a few miles from Amesbury, that, on the 24th of February 1284, she signed a grant of the Savoy to "her most dear son." * She enumerates in the barbarous Latin of the day, the " Domos, gardinum, placeas et redditus cum pertinentis suis," which she included in her gift, speaking of them as having been acquired from the provost and chapter of the house of Mountjoy, and as having been previously the property of " her

* For a copy of the grant, see Appendix.

most dear uncle," Peter, Count of Savoy. Thus,
then, a connection was established between the
Honour of Lancaster and the manor of the
Savoy, which has subsisted until the present
day.

Of Earl Edmund's tenancy there is but little
to be recorded. That little is founded on
tradition, inference, heraldry, and other elements
of bad history, yet it must find a place, and a
prominent one, in our pages. But an authentic
paper comes first.

Having on the 21st June 1293 obtained the
King's licence to crenellate or fortify his house,
he proceeded to build round it for protection
"a wall," so we read, "of stone and lime
(*de petra et calce*)," and thus, no doubt, the Savoy
began to wear the aspect in which it was
familiar to Chaucer and Wycliffe, to the Black
Prince and his prisoner, the King of France, to
John Froissart and John of Gaunt, and under
which its glories as a palace may be said to
have culminated. How much more Earl Edmund did we cannot tell, but this licence is of
especial use to us, as enabling us to strengthen
our previous impressions as to the house
originally built by Count Peter. A few years
before, Edward the First had (17th Aug. 1285)
confirmed his brother in his possessions, re-
capitulating in his charter the grant to Peter,

the sale by the "Domus Pauperum" of Mount-joy, and the gift by Queen Eleanor.

In 1296, about Whitsuntide, the Earl of Lancaster, to whom Poitou had been granted in 1291, died at Bayonne. He had besieged Bordeaux in the previous year without success ; and his death may have been partly caused by his disappointments and losses. His body was brought to England, and interred in his father's noble church at Westminster, where the body of his first wife, Aveline de Fortibus, already reposed. Their tombs are among the most remarkable in the Abbey. That of the countess is usually reckoned the earliest in the Pointed style which it contains ; it is separated from the monument of her husband by that of Aymer de Valence,* and the three occupy the whole north side of the Sacrarium.

The connection of Earl Edmund with the government of his father's and brother's kingdom was always of an intimate kind ; but in Memorials of the Savoy he deserves a place for a reason very different from any afforded by his public career. It has always been asserted that on his return home from the East he

---

* Aymer's father was step-brother to Henry III. Dean Stanley unaccountably speaks of him as the nephew of Earl Edmund. The Earl was nephew to William de Valence, and cousin to Aymer.

brought from Provence some plants of those red roses which afterwards became the cognizance of his descendants, and which, as Dean Stanley remarks, are still to be seen carved upon his monument. It must have been to his garden in the Savoy that these plants were first conveyed. The gardens there were already remarkable; and a new significance is given to the famous scene in the Temple Gardens, by remembering that not far off, on the same slope, were, in all probability, first seen in England the beautiful flowers now so long and so closely connected with her history. Irishmen love to trace the shamrock to St. Patrick. Scotsmen have their appropriate legend to account for the thistle of King James. But the story of the roses which bloomed in the garden of the Savoy when Earl Edmund came home from the Crusade is wholly unknown, or else forgotten by Englishmen. Shakspeare * has immortalised the white and red roses which bloomed in the Temple Gardens a hundred and fifty years after the time of Earl Edmund; but it is not presuming too much on historical probabilities to trace their origin on the banks of the Thames to that other garden, a little higher up the stream, in which they were first planted when Edmund of Lancaster brought

* *Henry VI.*, Part I. act ii. sc. 4.

The Earls
of Lan-
caster.
"Saint"
Thomas of
Lancaster.

them home with his bride from the sunny pleasances of Provence.

Earl Edmund having died in 1296, his eldest son, Thomas, succeeded him in his titles. We do not hear much about him for some years after the death of his father. It is probable he wanted some years of being of age, but exact information of the date of his birth has not been obtained. He accompanied his uncle, King Edward, in his Scottish campaigns, and in the fourth year after the accession of his cousin, Edward the Second, he married the Lady Alice de Lacy, daughter of that Earl of Lincoln whose name still remains in his town house not far from the Savoy. The year after his marriage we find him continuing to the Bishop of Llandaff the grant of a piece of ground in the Strand which his father, Earl Edmund, had first made, and several other grants and leases occur in the following years, proving his possession of the Savoy, but beyond these we have no evidence of his residing there, and nothing in particular to connect his name with it. He obtained from Aymer de Valence, Earl of Pembroke, the quit rents and other rights he had held in the "New" Temple, as it was then called, to distinguish it from the old Temple in Holborn, then still standing; and in the document of conveyance, which is in French, and the confirmation by the King, which is in Latin, Earl Thomas is set forth in full as Earl of Lancaster and of Leicester, Seneschal of England. It thus appears that he had succeeded his father in his great office, as well as in his earldoms. The inheritance was destined to be of greater importance a hundred years later. Lady Alice was but a child. Her father died in 1312, and her husband was henceforth at the head of his party. In the opposition which the English nobles offered to the favourites of Edward the Second, his part is well known, and is a matter of general history. His action led to the banishment of Gaveston in 1308, and he was again driven to extreme measures when the favourite returned from Flanders. Edward was at York, and there his beloved Gaveston repaired. But, without much delay or hesitation, the Earl of Lancaster assembled his forces and marched to York, only to find that Edward and Gaveston had retreated to Newcastle. There, too, he followed them, when they embarked and came back as far as Scarborough. Edward left his favourite in the castle of that place, and made for York, but Lancaster concentrated his attention on Gaveston alone, and speedily laying siege to Scarborough Castle, forced him to surrender. He was taken to Warwick, and beheaded with little ceremony on Blacklow

Hill. This was in 1312, and the document mentioned above as relating to the Temple, was signed by Edward at York on the first of October 1314, from which it seems likely that Lancaster, notwithstanding the part he had taken against Gaveston, had contrived afterwards to make his peace with the King. Indeed, there is evidence that personally the weak Edward esteemed him highly.

How far he was concerned the same year in the disastrous battle of Bannockburn we do not pause to inquire. His influence with the King was exerted in August 1315 in a matter of entirely peaceful importance, if to him is owing the issue of a precept signed by Edward at Langley, where he had a hunting-seat, of an

ordinance for the paving of the Strand. Since the commencement of our narrative this street had much increased in commercial importance. Several shops are spoken of in deeds and leases ; and, apparently, the number of people of the middle class had greatly increased. The dangerous and muddy track which led from Westminster, through "Charrynge" and St. Clement's to Temple Bar required constant repair, and Edward granted to four trustees the right of levying turnpike charges for the pavement of the highway.* The trustees are

* Rot. Pat. 9. Edwd. II. pt. i. m. 27, 8 Aug. 1315.

William de Layre, Richard Abbot, William le Roug, and Thomas Seman, all, we may suppose, tradesmen living in the street.

In the following year a fresh disagreement with King Edward was at full height. A reconciliation made by the mediation of the Pope was broken by the misconduct of the King, and after various events which belong to history, the opposition to Edward's new favourites, the Despensers, came to a head, and they were banished from the Kingdom. An insult offered to the Queen by the Badlesmere family caused a new combination among parties. The Queen, failing to obtain redress from Lancaster, threw her influence into the opposite scale, and Edward, strengthened by the support of his vigorous wife, was enabled in 1322 to recall his favourites. They proceeded at once to establish themselves by extreme measures against Lancaster, their chief opponent. They had the power in their hands for once, and they did not hesitate to use it to the utmost. A force, under the Earls of Surrey and Kent, was sent into the north against Lancaster, while the King himself marched into the west, where he broke up the forces of the Earl of Hereford and the Mortimers, and turning northward followed Hereford, who with his men had marched to join Lancaster. In the

The Earls of Lancaster.

meanwhile Lancaster, unfortunately for his good fame, had entered into negotiations with the Scots for assistance, and had taken up a position behind the Trent, where he awaited the King's onset, near Burton. The two armies, impeded by a flood, watched each other for several days, until Edward's soldiers found a ford, when Lancaster burnt Burton and retreated into Yorkshire. There was an unusual want of spirit and even of common sense in Lancaster's conduct at this time. He dispirited his soldiers by unnecessary retreat, while by his communications with Bruce he turned all true Englishmen against him. After some delay at Pontefract, he again commenced his retreat, but finding a force at Boroughbridge under the Governors of York and Carlisle, he attempted in vain to pass, and his associate, Hereford, having been killed, while no succour came from Scotland, he surrendered himself. On the body of Hereford proofs were found of the treasonable correspondence with the Scots, and Lancaster, doubly disgraced, was taken to Pontefract by the Sheriff, to whose custody the Governor of York, Sir Andrew Harcla, had committed him, and was tried by the King and his peers, and condemned. The pious ejaculations he made use of, and the memory of his former patriotic resistance to Gaveston and the

Despensers shed a kind of fictitious halo round the last scenes of his life. But it is difficult to see how Edward could have spared him. The extreme rigour of the sentence was indeed remitted. He was not hanged but beheaded, being taken to execution on a sorry nag with no bridle. The populace, even of his own town, jeered him. In his messages to the Scots, he had called himself "King Arthur," and the assumed title was applied to him now with all the accompaniments of solemn mockery. Whether from fear or from real piety, he cried aloud to Heaven, and in after years his prayers were quoted as evidence of his sanctity. To us, after so many ages, his conduct is only consistent with that of a fanatic, who mistakes his own delusions for religion, and who, when death overtakes him, forgets in the fervour of spasmodic devotion, a life passed in vanity and profligacy. Lancaster's execution took place on the 22d March 1322. Eight and twenty of his followers suffered at the same time.

The Earls of Lancaster.

Very soon after his death the tide of popular feeling turned in his favour. The rapacity of the Despensers renewed their unpopularity, and the Queen, although she had done nothing to save his life, now took part with those who lamented his fall. It is possible that she did not know of his fate till it had been decided.

Henry, Earl of Lancaster.

The Earls of Lancaster.

His brother Henry had become the head of the family, and he sided with her. The earldom and the estates had been forfeited by Earl Thomas's treason, but in March 1324, two years after his death, they were restored to Earl Henry. The widowed Countess Alice, whom Lancaster had neglected and even ill-treated, was in her own right called Countess of Lincoln and of Salisbury, and married twice after the Earl's death, but died without children in 1348.

St. Thomas of Lancaster.

The circumstances of Lancaster's death and the contradictory and inconsistent reports of his character had, almost immediately after the execution, invested him with all the qualities required to form a popular saint. His violence, his selfishness, his lust, his cruelty, his turbulence were all forgotten. His manly appearance, his princely liberality, his piety, his resistance to tyranny, his melancholy end,— these only were remembered, and a year had not elapsed before miracles were wrought at his tomb, and worshippers assembled to do honour to his memory, and to kneel before his picture hung up in St. Paul's. In June 1323* the King wrote to the Bishop of London, desiring him to restrain the people from the cult and adoration of a rebel, "and that too

* Reg. of Royal Charters ; Dy. of Lanc. iii. 28. De non accedendo ad quandam tabulam in Ecclesia Sti. Pauli.

without the authority of the Roman Church;"
and complaining that miracles were said to have
been wrought, commands the Bishop to exhort
the people against absurdities, as tending to
the dishonour of the Church.   But the King's
letter, which dates from York, had little effect.
" St. Thomas of Lancaster " soon vied with St.
Thomas of Canterbury in the devotion of the
people.   The archbishop had died for the
liberties of the Church, but the Earl for the
liberties of the people.   Hymns were composed
in his honour, or rather, in accordance with the
custom of the day, old hymns were parodied.
A manuscript in the British Museum* preserves
the " Office of St. Thomas of Lancaster," in
which the usual anthem, collect prose, and
sequence were provided.   The first lines, in imi-
tation of a hymn then in common use, ran as
follows :—

> " Gaude Thoma, ducum decus, Lucerna Lancastriæ,
>   Qui per necem imitaris Thomam Cantuariæ ;
>   Cujus caput conculcatur pacem ob Ecclesiæ,
>   Atque tuum detruncatur causa pacis Angliæ."

Some years later, after the deposition of
Edward, a serious attempt seems to have been
made to obtain the formal canonisation of Earl
Thomas from the Pope, and Isabella herself

* MS. Reg. 12. c. xvi. printed by Mr. Wright in his
volume of *Political Songs* for the Camden Society. 1839.

The Earls of Lancaster.

wrote to urge the petition. Her letter is dated in February 1327, and in it the Queen, in her son's name, recites the virtues of the Earl and repeats the stories of his miracles, begging that " such a candle should not be hidden under a bushel, but be set on a candlestick that its light might be the greater." The Pope refused the prayer of the petition, and nothing was done, though Isabella had gone so far as to make an arrangement with the monks of the Priory at Pontefract to endow a chapel on 'the hillock where Thomas had suffered, and to provide a chaplain. This document, which is dated in June of the same year, on the Vigil of Pentecost, does not seem to have produced any very distinct effect, and though the " cultus " of St. Thomas of Lancaster went on for many years, it was never directly authorised by the Church, and eventually died out. A few years later another turn in the tide of popular opinion sent crowds to worship at the tomb of the King by whose judgment Earl Thomas had been put to death.

Meanwhile the Savoy had been granted to Edward, Earl of Chester, as the King's eldest son was called. In this grant* the place is described as " that messuage with its appurtenances ' quod vocatur la Sauveye,' near the stone

* 14th July 1324. Rot. Pat. 18, Ed. II. pt. i. m. 35.

cross outside the Bar of the New Temple." Another document,* dated in 1326, gives us some further particulars, among which it is only worth while to note that Hugh le Despenser had a grant of that portion adjoining the Temple which Earl Thomas had obtained from Aymer de Valence, as already mentioned, and that the jury who made the inquisition found Henry, Earl of Lancaster, to be the next heir, and to be then forty years of age. He must, then, have been about nine at the time of his father's death in 1296. He bore the nickname of " Wryneck," on account, probably, of some physical peculiarity.†

Of Earl Henry there is little which we need pause to record. He took an active part in the revolution which deposed Edward II. and seated Edward III. on the throne, and having had the custody of "Sir Edward of Carnarvon" until his removal to Berkeley Castle, was tutor to the young King. The inquisition above named seems to have been made when he was admitted to his brother's titles and inheritance. It is to be presumed that he resided at the

The Earls of Lancaster.

The 3d Earl.

---

* Inquisitio post-mortem concerning the property of Thomas, Earl of Lancaster, Esc. 1. Edward III. No. 88.

† This surname has sometimes been applied to his son, the first duke. Miss Yonge gives it to both, perhaps by an error. *Cameos*, I. p. 351 and II. p. 73.

Savoy, but we have few records to connect him with it, and may briefly sum them up. In 1335 a somewhat mysterious occurrence took place at the Savoy. We learn by a Commission* issued on the 10th July that some "malefactors" got into the garden of Henry, Earl of Lancaster, "in the parish of St. Clement Danes, without the Bar of the New Temple," and digging by night under a pear tree, found a certain treasure and carried it off, but what it was, and how much, and whither they took it, does not appear. A jury was directed to inquire into the matter, but if anything was found out it has not been placed on record. The treasure-trove was said to have been of no small value (*ad valorem non modicum*), but that is all we know and, very possibly, exaggerated rumour will account for the whole affair.

Earl Henry obtained in 1342 a curious charter† from the King, in which extraordinary privileges and immunities were granted to him and his heirs. He was to have freedom from all tolls throughout the kingdom, from writs and summons, attachment of pleas, jurisdiction of sheriffs; from fines, forfeitures, waste, and in fact from all those exactions which in the

* Rot. Pat. 9. Ed. III., Pt. 2, m. 27d.

† 7 May 1342. Rot. Cart. 16. Ed. III. No. 11.

fourteenth century were so profitable a source
of revenue to the Crown.   The Earl probably
enjoyed these exceptional liberties until his
death, but we find, from an ` endorsement or
memorandum, dated in September 1349, they
were surrendered by his successor, as being, in
the opinion of the King and his council, made
to the loss of his King and the injury of the
royal inheritance, and were regranted for one
life only.

The Earl of Lancaster had a son and five
daughters by his wife, Maud, the daughter and
heiress of Sir Patrick Chaworth.   Of the
daughters one became Countess of Ulster, and
eventually mother-in-law to Lionel, Duke of
Clarence.   Another was the wife of the Earl of
Arundel, and the youngest, Isabel, was prioress
of the great convent in which her grandmother,
Queen Eleanor, had been a nun.

Earl Henry died in 1345, and was buried at
Leicester.

CHAPTER III.

The First Duke of Lancaster.

Henry, First Duke—The County Palatine—The Strand
and its Pavement—A Strand Jury in 1356—John,
King of France, at the Savoy—His Death—The
Duke of Lancaster's Heirs.

WHEN Henry, Earl of Lancaster, died in 1345,
he was peaceably succeeded by his only son,
who was called after him. He had already, as
Earl of Derby, taken his seat among the peers,
and was constantly employed in the Scottish and
French wars. His public acts are noticed here
only so far as they connect him with the history
of the Savoy. It will be sufficient to state in
addition, that he held a very distinguished
position even before his father's death, that he
married Isabel, daughter of Henry Lord
Beaumont, and that in 1351, proceeding to
Prussia to fight against the heathen, he was
taken prisoner by the Duke of Brunswick and

made to pay a ransom of 300 crowns for his release.

Meanwhile he had added to his possessions in the Strand. In 1347 and the three following years we find several records of purchases. Now it was a shop, again it was a house. Sometimes he extended his boundary towards the east, sometimes towards the north. The garden of the Abbot of Westminster (Covent Garden) is spoken of as a limit,* and the parishes of St. Mary "de la Stronde" and of St. Clement Danes, "without the Bar of the New Temple," are frequently named. In 1350† all the lands and houses of Sir Henry le Scrop, or Scrope, in both parishes were obtained and added to the manor of the Savoy, which now by degrees assumed the dimensions it has since preserved. The amount of one purchase may be estimated from the fact that a document is still extant in which William de Alyngton, clerk, acting for Sir Henry Scrope, acknowledges, on behalf of his employer, the sum of £30, from Sir Henry de Walton, archdeacon of Richmond, who was treasurer of the Earl of Lancaster.

Eleven months later Henry, the fourth Earl, became the first Duke of Lancaster. The letters patent are dated the 6th of March 1351.

The First Duke of Lancaster.

Henry, First Duke.

* Reg. xi. 24. Nov. 18, 1348.
† *Ibid.* 20th April, 21st April, and 24th April, 1350.

The First Duke of Lancaster

The King creates Henry, Earl of Lancaster, Duke of Lancaster with the assent of parliament, and empowers him, for life, to hold a Court of Chancery in the county, to appoint justices, and to exercise all other liberties and rights belonging to the county Palatine which were exercised by the Earl of Chester in the county of Chester, reserving only to the Crown the taxes and subsidies granted by parliament or the clergy, or imposed on the clergy by the Holy See : such taxes are to be collected by the Duke's officers, but the King is to have power of pardon for "life or members," and for the correction of errors in the Duke's courts : and the Duke is to send two knights to parliament from the county, as well as two burgesses from every borough.

The County Palatine.

It is from this time that the Savoy has been the head-quarters, so to speak, of the great Duchy Palatine of Lancaster. Within the precinct the offices of the Chancery are still situated, having been rented from the Master and Chaplains during the time when the Hospital existed, and it is in virtue of the present identification of the Sovereign of these Kingdoms with the possessor of the Duchy that the chapel of St. John, which, as we shall presently see, was probably already in existence, has become a "Chapel Royal."

The Savoy had now arrived at the highest point in its history. It was constantly visited by the kings and princes, by the knights and nobles, by the poets and prelates, whose lives go to make the history of the reign of Edward the Third. But Chaucer and Froissart and Wycliffe could not protect it by their genius. The Black Prince and his brothers, great as they were, had to bow before the social pressure of the times, and the years of a single generation had not elapsed when all was in ruin.

The First Duke of Lancaster.

Meanwhile the old question as to the pavement of the Strand comes up again. In 1353 the roadway was worse than ever, as the traffic was greater. On the 20th of November the King issued a patent to John de Bedeford, in which a melancholy account of the state of the pavement is given in Latin, the most debased we have almost ever seen in a serious document. The King observes that whereas the highway, "alta via," which leads from Temple Bar to the Abbot's Gate at Westminster, has become deep and muddy, "profunda et lutosa," owing to the constant passage back and forwards of carts and horses, "tam carectarum quam equorum," bearing "mercandisas et victualia," for the market at Westminster, "Stapulum;" and whereas the pavement is so deteriorated and broken that it may not easily be

The Strand and its Pavement.

The First Duke of Lancaster. mended, great danger is likely to ensue for both men and carriages, "tam hominibus quam cariagiis;" a toll is levied on the goods brought to market, and a schedule of articles taxed is added. John de Bedeford is entrusted with the organisation and proper application of the tolls, which were to be taken on all goods, whether coming by land or water. The application of the money thus gathered, and the enforcement of the rule already commanding every householder to take care of the pavement as far as the channel or kennel (canellus) in front of his own door, do not seem to have mended the Strand roadway very effectually, and in a few years we have the question brought up once more. In 1359, and again in 1361, commissions on the subject were issued, the tolls being appointed for one year at a time, and gradually the system thus introduced seems to have got into working order, so that some years elapsed before we hear of any more complaints.

Another little arrangement, made about the same time, may be noticed here. We have already seen that the Strand had become more and more populous since the days of Count Peter. The line of houses on either hand was now probably continuous, or broken only by the long walls and entrance gateways of those bishops and nobles who had palaces outside Temple Bar. This increase of the population necessitated an increase of church accommodation, not so much for the living as for the dead. The dangerous, and indeed hideous, custom of intramural burial had not yet been charged with those visitations of pestilence to which London was then and for centuries after so often exposed. In 1355 a licence was obtained from the King, at Woodstock, permitting the Duke to grant a piece of land "placeam terræ," seventy feet in length and thirty in breadth, to John de Branketre, parson of the church of St. Mary, "personæ ecclesiæ," for the enlargement of the cemetery. For this licence six shillings and eight-pence were demanded and paid, and in the following year we find an inquiry on the subject, when, a jury having been impanelled at the Stone Cross in the Strand, it was decided that the enlargement had been effected without any damage to the King or his subjects, the piece of ground having been duly measured, and being situated at a distance from human habitations. A gateway with a room over it had, it seems, been erected, but where this gateway, which may have been a kind of lych gate, stood, we have no means now of discovering. The cemetery, like the church, was on the site now covered by Somerset House.

But this inquisition is interesting for another reason. It gives the names, as we may suppose, of some of the respectable inhabitants and rate-payers of the district. The Royal Escheator, who held the inquiry, was attended, so we read, by, among others, Walter *Barbour*, Hugh *Glover*, Henry *Taillour*, William *Pynner*, Alexander *Fourriere*, and Geoffrey *Goldbeter;* just, in fact, such a gathering of tradesmen as we should still expect to find on a jury or vestry in any of the fashionable suburbs of our present London. Tailors, glovers, and barbers would flourish among so many great houses, and we cannot doubt that in some cases, if not in all, these names actually represent the callings of the persons to whom they belonged.

Both furnishers and decorators, whether of men or mansions, had, we may be certain, a busy time in the spring of 1357. The King and his son had gained a great victory in France ; they had even taken prisoner the King of France, and the citizens were determined to welcome them on their return with all the magnificence in their power. Froissart* gives some account of the entry of the captive King and the Black Prince, and mentions, among other things, that John rode on a white steed with very rich furniture, while the young prince

* Johnes's *Froissart*, 1. 172.

accompanied him on a "little black hackney." When they had attended the King of England at Westminster, they returned and alighted at the Savoy, and there the King of France was lodged at first. The King of England, Edward III. visited him in the Savoy, accompanied by Queen Philippa, and both entertained him sumptuously, and also, as Froissart quaintly says, "consoled him all in their power." How the Duke of Lancaster liked this invasion of his house we do not know. He was absent at the abortive siege of Rennes, and before long, we know, John was removed to Windsor Castle, where he was permitted to hunt and hawk, while his lords, who remained in London, presumably in the Savoy, were allowed on parole to go back and forward to visit him.

Although another Duke owned the Savoy before the French King's captivity was ended by death, it may be convenient to sum up the rest of the story here, so far, at least, as the Savoy is concerned in it.

It is well known that King John was allowed to return to France in 1360. His ransom was to be three million crowns, besides the cession of Aquitaine. His release took place on the 25th October, when the first instalment was paid. His two younger sons became his hostages at Calais, while twenty young French nobles were sent to London. Among them was the Sire de Coucy, who afterwards married the Lady Isabel, eldest daughter of King Edward. John's endeavours to raise the rest of the ransom were not successful, and he determined to return to England. Various accounts have been given of his motives. The favourite version represents him as dispirited by the condition of his country, and impelled by the doubly honourable desire not to make her burden greater, as well as to fulfil his promise to Edward. A second account connects his return to England with the visit of the King of Cyprus, who had already been here, anxious to arrange for a crusade in which both John and Edward, as well as the Kings of Scotland and Denmark, were to join. But there were not wanting some who saw the matter in a different light, and attributed to King John motives of a very disgraceful kind. According to one of the Chroniclers,* from the time of his first arrival he had employed persons secretly to collect, both in London, and other places throughout England, the "choice gold," and to pack it in iron-bound cases and convey it to France. Moreover, according to the same authority, he had gathered together weapons of war, especially bows and arrows, and had concealed as

---

* Knighton, *Col.* 2627.

many as a thousand bows in bales of wool for exportation at a convenient opportunity.

Soon after his return, and before the scheme of a united crusade, or indeed any of the projects which may reasonably be presumed to have occupied his mind had time to be matured, he fell ill. He had visited Edward and Philippa at Eltham, and had been honourably received by the citizens of London, and the Savoy had a second time been assigned to him for a residence. His illness does not seem to have lasted many days; but from its alarming nature, it caused considerable uneasiness in several quarters. One of his French attendants, the Sieur de Boucicaut, crossed to France to convey the news to John's son, the Regent. There were other potentates also who were variously affected, and Froissart enters at some length into the schemes and arrangements of the King of Navarre and others in anticipation of the King's death. Meanwhile his illness became greater, and the physicians despaired of his life. According to the *Chronicle* from which we quoted above* he sent for King Edward, as he felt death approaching, and acknowledged to him the treasonable designs he had entertained. Nor was this all, for, according to the same account, he further confessed that he held the

* Knighton, 2627.

crown of France illegally and unjustly. King Edward, with his habitual magnanimity, forgave him, but we read that, with equally characteristic vigilance, he ordered the arrest and punishment of the Englishmen who had assisted in collecting the money and arms.

And so John of Valois died at the Savoy, and King Edward made him a great funeral, and had masses performed in divers places, himself following the corpse for some miles as it took the road to Dover. It was in due time conveyed to St. Denis, and was buried there on 7th of May 1364, being just a month, all but one day, after the captive King had died.

Nearly three years before this event the Duke of Lancaster had died, but not at his mansion in the Strand. The plague, then fatally prevalent throughout England, seized him at Leicester in 1361; and on Easter Eve (March 27) he died. His body was buried, like his father's, at Leicester, and his great inheritance descended to his two daughters, for he had no son. An inquisition was held at St. Mary's in the Strand, two months later, by the king's escheator, William de Hatton, when it was found that his heirs were his two daughters, Matilda, who is described as twenty-one years of age, and "Blanchia," who was nineteen.

This inquisition,* like one noticed above, is especially interesting as giving us the names of the jurors or witnesses assembled to try the matter. They were, we read, John Wantyngge, William Lovel, John Corsoun, William Walbere, Richard Wardok, John Gate, alias John of Lancastreshyre, Thomas Carpenter, Barthram Forvour, John Cordewaner, Walter Senpre, and Walter Barbour.

A year had hardly elapsed when a second inquiry of the same kind was held, not in the Strand, but at Westminster. The Duke's eldest daughter, the Lady Maud, or Matilda, young as she was, had been twice married before her father's death. Her first husband was the eldest son of Lord Stafford, and her second William Count of Holland and Zealand, called in the document † before us, Duke of Bavaria. She died, leaving no children, on Palm Sunday (10th April 1362), and the jurors found that the inheritance had not yet been divided, and that her sister Blanche, the wife of John, " Earl of Richmond," was now heir to the whole of it.

* *Inquis. p. m.*, Ed. III., pt. i., 122.
† *Inquis. p. m.*, Ed. III., pt. i., No. 37.

CHAPTER IV.

John of Gaunt.

Earl of Richmond—Duke of Lancaster—The Manor House—The Chapel—The Kitchen—The Garden—Chaucer—The first Chancellor—Duke John's Marriages.

WE hardly recognise John of Gaunt under the title of "Earl of Richmond." But it is the designation he bore for twenty years, from 1342 until the Dukedom of Lancaster was conferred on him in 1362. His wife, as we have seen, inherited the whole of her father's estates on the death of her sister in April of that year; and the elevation of John, her husband, to the dukedom followed, almost as a matter of course. The creation bears date the 13th November, and in the notice of it in the Rolls of Parliament, he is called "Earl of Lancaster,* a dignity to which he could only

Courthope's *Nicolas,* p. 278.

have succeeded in right of his wife, under the charter of 30th June 1267." In 1372 he resigned the Earldom of Richmond.

With the eventful history of John of Gaunt we have nothing to do in these pages, except so far as it relates to the Savoy. During his earlier years he was constantly employed abroad; but the Savoy was kept in repair even during his absence, and was his London residence when he attended parliament. We give in the appendix* summaries of several documents relating to this period; but in endeavouring to convey some idea both of the appearance presented by the residence itself, and of the great events of which it was the scene, we must abandon a strictly chronological method, and proceed on a plan calculated better to save trouble to the reader and to ourselves.

Although no contemporary view of the Savoy, or even of the Strand, in the fourteenth century, has come down to us, we may form a tolerably accurate idea of the kind of house Duke John and his court inhabited; and by comparing our idea, thus formed, with what we know of the site, we may approximate, by no means remotely, to an understanding of the real appearance of the place. The records to which we have had access relate chiefly to two features of the

* See Appendices C, D, E, F.

John of Gaunt.

Savoy; one of them actually survives, and the other is embalmed in the immortal verse of Chaucer. The gardens and the chapel are frequently mentioned.

The Manor House.

The house of John of Gaunt, in all probability, consisted, like the other great houses of the day, of a quadrangle or series of quadrangles, surrounded by domestic buildings. There was a great gateway, half fortified and protected by a portcullis, facing the Strand. This gate was probably on the site now marked by Savoy Street, and occupied the centre of the Strand front. A smaller gate or postern for foot passengers only, may have been at one side, and the space between was guarded by a long line of wall, pierced with a few windows at some distance from the ground, and serving to mask the residences of the soldiers and lower rank of retainers with which the court of every great man's house was in those days filled. Entering by the great gate we should have seen, on the right the chapel, and in front, probably the great hall, a prominent feature in every nobleman's house. The private apartments were beyond the hall, between it and the river on which they looked out, pleasant terraces intervening, with gardens and orchards extending to the water's edge. There was, of course, a landing-place or "stairs," as the river was in those days the great thoroughfare, with low houses for the Duke's barges, and sheds or cloisters for the bargemen to wait in. The kitchen adjoined the hall, probably running at right angles to it, and, if so, occupying the left-hand side of the courtyard, that, namely, facing the chapel. Farther than this we must not go in our conjectural restoration; but in forming an idea of the size and splendour of the place, we may remember the names of the buildings which had to find room, and may appropriate space as we please for the Chancery of the Duchy, for the wine vaults, for the library, for the treasure-chamber, and for many other rooms, as well as stables and boat-houses, which are mentioned or referred to in contemporary documents. There was little attempt at fortification, notwithstanding the licence to "crenellate," granted as we saw in 1293; the rioters broke in with ease in 1376, and the rebels at the final destruction in 1381; yet in outward appearance the Savoy had probably much resemblance to what in these days would be called a castle, battlemented walls, tall towers, small windows, and an abundance of loop-holes and machicolations.

The only allusion to the kitchen which is worth noticing among the many account books and registers still in existence, is an amusing

John of Gaunt.

warrant, dated the 20th December 1372, and very suggestive of approaching Christmas festivities on a large scale. This document commences in the usual form "Johan, par le Grace de Dieu," and so on, and is addressed, "à nostre quarrenner," to our warrener at Aldbourne; it then proceeds, "we charge and command you that you catch as quickly as you can five dozen of the best and fattest rabbits (les plus bones et grosses coniz) in our warren, in such wise that they may be at our manor of the 'Sauvoye' on next Friday without any default or excuse."

The Garden.

Besides rabbits and the means of supplying them, we have some information as to the arrangements the Duke made for vegetables. His agreement is extant with Nichol Gardiner, whose occupation appears by his surname; and from it we learn that the modern system in many great gardens by which the gardener is allowed to pay himself out of the sale of surplus fruit is at least five hundred years old. The document commences by an undertaking to pay Nichol the sum of twopence daily, *pour ces gages*, and further ordains that he is to have all manner of fruits and vegetables growing in the said garden to make his own profit from, saving to the Duke that which is needful for the use of his household as occasion may arise. Further we read that the said Nichol is to manure and work (*maniourera et ovrera*) the said gardens at his own costs and charges, providing for the purpose all things needful (*busoignables*), except that the Duke will find him rails and borders in the time of railing (*railles et verges en temps de raillement*); and the agreement ends with a precept to the receiver-general to pay to Nichol his daily twopence, and to make him such additional payment for rails as may be considered right by " our beloved clerk, Sir John de Yerdeburgh, of our wardrobe."*

Seeing the Duke paid such wages to his gardener, for twopence a day was no inconsiderable sum in the fourteenth century, we may expect to find, and, as we shall see, actually do find that the gardens were well kept up. We have already spoken of the introduction of the Provence rose by the first Earl of Lancaster : but gardening had much improved since those days. The estimation in which it was held, and the appearance of gardens at the period may be learnt from the poetry of Chaucer; poetry the more appropriate to the present purpose, because we know that the Savoy was a constant resort of his ; that at least one of his poems relates to the Duchess of Lancaster; that there he won the hand of the fair Philippa

* 30th June 1312. Register Temp., Ed. III., f. 154.

Roet; and, what is perhaps of more importance
to us, that it was out of the revenues of the
manor of the Savoy that the pension of £10
a year granted him by the Duke, was paid.
The value of this pension may be more easily
estimated by remembering that the salary of a
judge was, in those days, £26 : 13 : 4. Chaucer
had, therefore, besides the friendship of the
Duke and Duchess, good cause to remember the
Savoy, and to the poem known as *Chaucer's
Dream* an allegory relating to the loves of
John of Gaunt and Blanche of Lancaster, whose
marriage took place in 1359, we naturally look
for descriptions from which to form an idea of
the Savoy and its surroundings.

In quoting we venture, as far as possible, to
modernise the spelling for our readers' convenience; but the original is so easily accessible
that no apology seems to be needed. Almost
at the opening of the poem we have a description which might fit the manor-house in the
Strand :—

> " Within an isle methought I was,
> Where wall and gate was all of glass
> And so was closed round about
> That leave less none come in nor out,
> Uncouth and strange to behold
> For every gate of fine gold,
> A thousand vanes, aye turning,
> Entuned had and birds singing

Diverse : and on each vane a pair,
With open mouths against the air.
And of a suite were all the towers,
Subtly carven after flowers
Of uncouth colours, during aye,
That never been none seen in May,
With many a small turret high."

These vanes, many-coloured and many-shaped,
are characteristic of mediæval domestic architec-
ture, as portrayed in illuminated manuscripts.

Since the modern system of treating Chaucer
as Shakspeare has been treated for years past, has
come into vogue, a writer not specially learned
in his poetry, and especially one unacquainted
with the latest theories on the text of each poem,
has considerable hesitation in selecting passages
for quotation. But even as we cannot be sure
that Chaucer wrote any given poem, so neither
can we affirm positively that in any poem the
Savoy is referred to ; but this we may assert,
namely, that in several contemporary poems,
and notably in those which went by Chaucer's
name until lately, there are descriptions likely
to suit such a building as the Duke of Lancaster's manor-house was at its best. The poem
entitled the *Boke of the Duchesse, or the Dethe of
Blanche,* does even more. It describes for us
the fair lady who brought the Savoy and the
Duchy to Duke John, and to it we must refer

John of Gaunt. readers desirous of learning how lovely, good, and fair she was, and how much her death, in 1369, was lamented. Near the commencement a chamber is described, which may well have been one of those in the Savoy :—

> " And sooth to say my chamber was
> Full well depainted, and with glass
> ˙Were all the windows well yglazed
> Full clear   .   .   .
> And all the walls with colours fine
> Were painted, both text and gloss,
> And all the Romance of the Rose.
> My windows were shut, each one,
> And through the glass the sun shone."

Several other interiors might also be quoted. The following lines from the *Court of Love*, describe the exterior of a Gothic castle, but they have usually been taken to refer to one situated in a more genial climate than that of England :—

> " For I beheld the towers high and strong,
> And high pinnacles, large of height and long,
> With plate of gold bespread on every side,
> And precious stones, the stonework for to hide."

But the interior, allowing for poetical exaggerations, may suit our purpose :—

> —— " An hall of noble apparel
> With arras spread, and cloth of gold, I guess,
> And other silk of easier avail :
> Under the cloth of their estate, sans fail
> The King and Queen there sat, as I beheld."

Of the gardens too, we find many notices in Chaucer. All cannot relate expressly to the gardens of the Savoy. But some certainly, or almost certainly do, and of them some are very like what we have good reason to suppose the gardens of Middlesex were in Chaucer's day. This is from the *Assembly of Fowls* :—

> " A garden saw I full of blossomed bowis
> Upon a river in a green mead,
> There as sweetness evermore enow is,
> With flowers, white, blue, yellow, and red,
> And cold well streams, nothing dead,
> That swommen full of small fishes light,
> With fins red, and scales silver bright."

Of the trees of the surrounding park he has spoken in a previous verse :—

> " The builder oak and eke the hardy ash,
> The pillar elm, the coffer to carraine (*carrion*)
> The box pipe tree, holm to whip's lash,
> The sailing fir, the cypress death to plain ;
> The shooter yew, the aspe (n) for shafts plain,
> The olive of peace, and eke the drunken vine,
> The victor palm, the laurel, too, divine."

Similar descriptions occur in the *Flower and the Leaf:* but perhaps the most elaborate is in the *Complaint of a Lover's Life.* A river of water " clear as beryl or crystal," conducts the poet " towards a park, enclosed with a wall in compass round, and by a gate small, whoso that would freely might go

> Into this park walled with green stone."

He describes the soil within as "plain, smooth, and wonder soft," and as being all overspread with tapestry that nature had made herself : and finds there Daphne "closed under rind," and green laurel, pine, myrrh, cedars, filberts, hawthorn, ash, fir, and oak "with many a gouny acorn,

> And many a tree more than I can tell."

That John of Gaunt kept a kind of royal court at the Savoy in the closing years of Edward's life is abundantly evident. He constantly called himself the "King of Castile and Leon," and was, no doubt, addressed in full regal style. In the last year of his father's life he appointed an officer whose title and duties still survive, after the lapse of five hundred years. The chancellor of the Duchy of Lancaster, under Queen Victoria, is a minister of the Crown. The Duke of Lancaster had already, as early as 1360, a chancellor of his household. He was only a superior officer over the servants and tenants. But the Duke obtained, on the 28th February 1377, a licence from the King to have a chancery for his duchy. He may be said to have granted this licence to himself, for King

Edward was now in his dotage, and Duke John *John of* was practically regent of the kingdom. His *Gaunt.* royal father died in the following summer, so that the grant of this licence is one of the last acts of importance in his reign. By it the Duke is empowered to appoint a chancellor for his County of Lancaster, as well as justices for pleas of the crown and common pleas : and to send up two knights to parliament for the county palatine, and two burgesses for every borough. The Duke lost little time in selecting his first chancellor. From the memorandum of his appointment, of which I subjoin a copy,* it will be seen how great the Duke's position then was, and how important he intended the office to be. The first chancellor, Thomas de Thelwall, was sworn in the chapel, being himself a priest, and this is one of the earliest direct notices I find of the chapel. Whether it was the same chapel as that which stands now in the precinct, is a question not very easy to answer, but this would seem to be the proper place in which to put before the reader a few particulars regarding it.

It has, of course, been an interesting question The to determine whether the present chapel is in- Chapel. deed that in which John of Gaunt worshipped, whether, therefore, Wycliffe may have preached

* See Appendix B, from *Duchy of Lanc. Records,* class xxv. A. 6.

there, and Chaucer there have praised God. Unfortunately, only one solitary fact, one on which too much reliance must not be placed, exists to enable us to suppose that the present chapel is identical with that which stood in the Savoy in the time of Duke John. It is recorded that a certain John Sampull was buried there in 1510. Now, an adjoining monument to that of Sampull speaks of the burial of Humphrey Summerset as taking place in the chapel in 1515, and as being the first "since they it sacrated." From which we may infer that there was a burial-place here before the building of the chapel, or possibly the rebuilding, when the hospital was founded. It is very possible, even if the chapel of John of Gaunt was burnt by the rebels in 1381, that the walls and site remained, and were used for burials occasionally, until John Sampull was laid there in 1510, until a fresh chapel was consecrated on the old spot, and until Humphrey Summerset was buried in the newly "sacrated" ground. There are a few other considerations, which, though they can hardly be dignified with the name of reasons, yet tend to confirm the opinion thus hesitatingly put forward. The chapel is dedicated to St. John the Baptist, whom John of Gaunt reckoned as his patron saint. There is no reason Henry VII. should have specially selected

St. John for the patron of a new chapel, whereas the fact that the ruined chapel on the site was dedicated to St. John would weigh much in favour of a rededication to the same saint. And there is a further, and perhaps more important consideration to be taken into the account. In laying out the hospital there was absolutely no reason why the chapel should not be placed according to the almost invariable custom of the time, east and west. But the chapel of the Savoy stands north and south, the chancel window looking almost due north. The easiest way to account for this anomaly is to suppose that a previous chapel stood on the same site; that this previous chapel, being a private building, and the successor, possibly of a mere oratory, or praying-closet, in the old manor-house, stood, for convenience, north and south rather than east and west; and that when Henry's hospital came to be built it was thought best to use the old site, notwithstanding its unusual position, and to build, or rebuild, or restore the old Chapel of John of Gaunt on its original place, a place to some extent, at least, hallowed by interments during the time which intervened between the destruction of the palace and the founding of the hospital.

Of the chapel, as it was under John of Gaunt, we have a few notices. There are several occasions on which we read that the vestments or vessels belonging to the chapel were removed for a time. In 1372 the Chaplain, William de Burgh, receives 100 shillings, being his yearly salary. A little later John de " Segovoy," perhaps Segovia, is spoken of as dean of the Duke's chapeL In 1374 the sum of ten marks is paid for a missal for the chapeL A little earlier there is a record of the payment of 46s. 8d. for a primer with matins and psalms, but it is not clear that they were for the Savoy. There is a warrant extant, addressed to John de " Seggevoux, Dean de nostre chapelle," desiring him to. deliver certain things to Sir Lambert de Trykyngham " guardian of our chapel in the approaching voyage," for the Duke's use while he was away from home.*

* This is a list of the articles :—" un chalice ove la patine d'argent surrorez (gilt) ; deux fioles (phials) d'argent ; un camparnole (bell) d'argent surrorez ; une pax brede d'argent surrorez ; un petite spersure (sprinkler) d'argent pour ewe benette (holy water) ; une boiste pour le corps de Nostre Seigneur ; un cheasible de drap de soy de lures et de colers ; deux albes ovesque les parrures de meisme la suyt ; deux stoles et deux fanons de la dite suyt ; une fronter pour l'auter desouz ; une autre fronter par desuis, de meisme la suyt, ou un crucifixe enbroude ; deux towilles pour lavater de la dite suyte ; un superaltare ; un missal ; deux ridels de soy ovesque les cordes ; deux seyntures ; un canavace et un supplice."—*Reg. Temp.* Ed. III. 193 b. 17th April 1373.

. As I am writing the history of the Savoy, and not that of the Duchy of Lancaster, I will not go farther into the list of chancellors than to observe how many men of eminence have held the office since the appointment of John de Thelwall, including More and Cecil, and in our own day Campbell and Lord Clarendon.

Among other warrants for payments to be made by the Duke's treasurer, there is one of 3s. 4d. to the "estrange bargemen" who rowed the Duke over from Lambeth to the Savoy on the occasion of the death (*obit.*) of the Countess of Arundel. This is dated 24th April 1373. There are many other payments of the kind entered, but the most interesting of them all is the grant of Chaucer's annuity. It is dated 13th June 1374, and as it is not very long we may give it in full :—

Johan *etc.* Faisons savoir que nous de nostre grace especial et pour la bone *etc.* que nostre bien ame Geffray Chaucer nous ad fait, et auxint pour la bon service que nostre bien ame Philippe sa femme ad fait a nostre treshonore dame et miere la Royne, que Dieu pardoigne, et a nostre tresame compaigne, la Royne, avons graunte au dit Geffray x.li. (£10) par an, a terme de sa vie, appendre annuelment le course de sa vie durant a nostre manoir de la Sauvoye presde Loundres, par les mayns de nostre Receivour

General qi ore est ou qi pour le temps serra, as termes de Saint Michel et de Pasques par ouelles porcions. En t. *etc.* Done *etc.* a Sauvoy presde Londres, le xiij jour de Juyn, l'an xlviij.

The pension was given for services rendered by Chaucer and his wife. There is not a word about poetry, unless an "etc." in the above copy may be taken to refer to some such unusual and not easily described service. The wife of the poet had been servant to Queen Philippa, and was now in the household of her daughter-in-law, the Duchess Constance, called also "la Royne" in the warrant. It was in her right that John of Gaunt claimed the crown of Castile and Leon, a claim which led him constantly to call himself "King" until he gave up the empty title on the marriage of his only daughter, by Constance, to her cousin, the real king of Castile, Henry III., who paid him thenceforth an annual pension.

Many of the entries of payments at this period are very curious. The establishment must have been maintained on a great scale. A few notes from the various warrants to the treasurer may be of interest after five hundred years. In addition to Chaucer's annuity, Walter Dysse the Duke's confessor, was paid £10 a year. John of Ypres "Chief de nostre Conseil" had an annual fee of 100 marks. William de Burgh, a chaplain, had 100 shillings. On Wednesday the 13th and on Saturday the 16th April 1372 we read of 12s. 6d. and of 10s. being distributed in alms. Payments are also made to musicians : 100 shillings a year each, is the amount mentioned in one account : 40 shillings, in another, for "les troys petites clercs de nostre dite chapelle," and in 1380, to certain minstrels "faisant leur ministralcie devant nous a Savoye," 33s. 9d. John de Schelton is porter of the Savoy in 1372. A payment to him of 7s. 6d. is recorded on the 6th May of that year. Two years later, in 1374, John Norton holds the office and receives a penny a day for his services in addition to twopence which he had previously received. There are payments for archers sent to the Duke from his stewards and agents in Needwood Forest and other places. The wardrobe, too, occupies a large space. To the treasurer of the wardrobe are directed orders to pay for a "soor" falcon, (*i.e.* one which has not moulted), the sum of 66 shillings and eightpence. This falcon is a present for Thomas Holland, probably the grandson of Joane, Princess of Wales, John of Gaunt's sister-in-law.

A most singular list of expenses occurs also at the commemoration of the Duke's first wife on the anniversary of her death. She died in 1369, and the list is dated 1374. She it is whom

Duke John's Marriages.

Chaucer has celebrated as Duchess Blanche. She was buried in St. Paul's "near the principal altar," the funeral sermon being preached by John of Swaffham, a Carmelite, bishop of Cloyne in Ireland, and afterwards of Bangor, who chose for his text the words (Psa. xlix. 10), "For he seeth that wise men die, likewise the fool and the brutish person perish, and leave their wealth to others." The Bishop was a great opponent of Wycliffe, and may have chosen this text purposely to displease the Duke, whose protection of Wycliffe afterwards caused so much offence.

The second wife of Duke John was, as we have seen, Constance, the daughter and co-heiress of Peter, King of Castile. She died in 1394, leaving an only child, Katharine, who married her cousin, Henry of Castile, as mentioned above. John had already found her a successor. This was the widow of Sir Hugh Swynford, Katharine, sister of Chaucer's wife. Both were the daughters of a certain knight of Hainault, Payne Roet by name, who was a herald and "Guienne King of Arms." She had already borne him four children, known in history under the surname of Beaufort, and in 1396 he married her, being three years and a month only before his death. She only survived him four years.

But long before his third marriage, the Savoy itself had ceased to exist.

CHAPTER V.

𝕿𝖍𝖊 𝕯𝖊𝖘𝖙𝖗𝖚𝖈𝖙𝖎𝖔𝖓 𝖔𝖋 𝖙𝖍𝖊 𝕾𝖆𝖛𝖔𝖞.

The Unpopularity of Duke John—The good Parliament
—The interrupted Feast—The murdered Priest—The
Savoy reprieved—The second Attack—Buried alive
— The Accursed Thing—The Manor House dis-
mantled.

THE unpopularity of John of Gaunt had become
very great when, in 1376, the so-called "Good
Parliament" assembled. The Duke had been
for a time what at the present day would be
called Prime Minister, or something like it.
His adherents had misgoverned the country,
and he had himself failed in the conduct of the
war with France. In the disputes which arose
about the doctrines of Wycliffe, the citizens, or
at least the mob, of London had sided with
Courtenay, their bishop. The protection which
John of Gaunt afforded to the reformer probably
saved his life; but it is by no means to be

concluded that the Duke shared the religious opinions of Wycliffe. The whole history of the contests in which these two names are connected forms no part of the narrative with which we are here concerned. But it is worth while to caution some readers against the error of supposing that the Duke was really influenced by Wycliffe's doctrines, or that anything but political expediency was obeyed in the course he took. His manner of life is condemned by the chroniclers with great unanimity. One of them * says quaintly that his "doings were ever contrary, for, as it is thought, he wanted the grace of God." No doubt this writer is prejudiced against the Duke on account of Wycliffe, for he refers to him as "thys sonne, therfor, of perdition." But there cannot be any great doubt of the extreme dissoluteness of the Duke's life.

The Good
Parliament.
    At the Good Parliament the Duke of Lancaster was stoutly opposed in the Commons by Peter de la Mare, their Speaker. His high-handed proceedings increased his unpopularity, and shortly afterwards, when Wycliffe was summoned before the Bishop of London at St. Paul's, the Duke attended with him, and threatened the bishop with personal violence. This indecency greatly incensed the populace,

* *Archæologia*, vol. xxii.

with whom the bishop was a favourite. On the following day a crowd assembled at the gates of the Savoy, clamouring for the Duke and his companion, Lord Percy, whom they would doubtless have torn to pieces in their rage. The Duke and Percy, however, had gone to dine with a rich foreigner, William de Ypres, in the city; and as they were about to sit down to eat oysters, we are told, a soldier burst in with news of the tumult. The Duke and his friend were so terrified that they rushed out at once, leaving their oysters untasted. They took a boat on the Thames, and, crossing immediately, sought refuge at Kennington, where the Princess of Wales and her youthful son, afterwards Richard II., were living. The Princess, hearing their story, comforted them as best she was able, and, owing to her influence with the citizens, she eventually made peace between them and her brother-in-law. Meanwhile the mob, having wrecked Percy's house, had assembled at the Savoy gate, when an unfortunate priest, coming along the Strand, was imprudent enough to ask of a bystander the meaning of the commotion. He was immediately told that the insurgents sought for the Duke and Lord Percy, to obtain from them the release of Peter de la Mare, who had been unjustly imprisoned. The priest, on hearing this, ventured to observe that Peter

The Destruction of the Savoy.

The interrupted feast.

The De-
struction
of the
Savoy.

The
murdered
Priest.

was a traitor, and should have been hanged long ago.

The crowd were excited to fury by those foolish words. Exclaiming with a terrific clamour that he was a partisan of the Duke's, and a traitor to England, and that his own speech was witness enough, they ran upon him and so ill-treated him that he died in a few days.

Meanwhile, news of the riot had been brought to the Bishop of London, who was also sitting down to dinner. Leaving the table, he hastened to the Savoy. The crowd was still gathering. The bishop besought the people to remember the sacredness of the season, for it was Lent, and exhorted them, "by the love of Christ," to desist from their sedition, promising to obtain their wishes for them. His words were so far successful that the mob dispersed; but the chronicler* asserts that had he not contrived thus to pacify them, both the Duke and Lord Percy would that day have lost either life or limb. As the people dispersed, however, they tore down the Duke's arms where they were hung in the neighbouring streets, and reversed them, in sign that he was a traitor, a proceeding which greatly incensed the Duke. One of his retainers, Sir Thomas Swinton, a Scot, having the temerity to ride through the

* *Harl. MS.*, 3634.

streets bearing the Duke's badge round his neck, was torn from his horse, and would have been murdered but for the timely assistance of the Mayor, who rescued him from his assailants and sent him safe to his master. It was an instructive sight to observe that others who had been similarly decorated by the Duke of Lancaster took the badges off and hid them in their pockets or up their sleeves.

So the Savoy was saved that time, but its doom approached. The bishop, and even the archbishop, could not save it at the next attack.

For the causes which led to the great insurrection of the peasants in 1381, I must refer to Mr. Green's *History of the English People.* I have only, in this place, to do with that wave of the tide which poured over London, and with that particular eddy which overwhelmed the Savoy.

It was on the 13th of June, a day consecrated in the calendar to the festival of the Corpus Christi. The insurgents were in possession of London. They had poured in vast numbers over the bridge, and spread like a flood through the city. So far little violence had been done. But the day was very hot; and the Londoners had in many places left their taps and cellars open. The country folk were not accustomed to wine, and the agitators within the city, men

The Destruction of the Savoy.

The Savoy reprieved.

The second attack.

*The De-
struction
of the
Savoy.*
of a better class, who hated the Duke of Lancaster, contrived to inflame them both with
drink and arguments to attack the Savoy. The
Duke was away in the north. A few of his
servants only remained in the town house.
The mob did not need much persuasion to
make the attack. They crowded about the
house on every side. They surged along the
Strand from Temple Bar. They probably
approached by water in boats from London
Bridge. The Londoners willingly assisted.
Some of them, we read, were afraid lest the
honour of burning the Duke's house should be
taken out of their hands, and hastened to set
fire to it wherever they could. They killed
Roger Leeche, the Duke's sergeant-at-arms,
who would have resisted, and who, we may
suppose, endeavoured to defend one of the
entrances. The wardrobe was a central object
of attack, and though the keeper contrived to
escape with the hangings of one bed, all the
rest were destroyed. William Appulton, a Grey
Friar, who was the Duke's physician, was found
in the house and killed. But the greatest loss
Buried
alive.
of life was on their own side. Horrible stories
were long circulated as to thirty-two men buried
alive. The cellars had proved too great a
temptation, and though the rebels loudly proclaimed that they were not thieves, and ruthlessly

destroyed all the valuables they could find, they seem to have thought it lawful to use the wine to quench their thirst. And so the story goes that a party of them, having entered the cellar, drank so much sweet wine that they could not come out, but, amusing themselves with jokes, songs, and other drunken pleasures, were imprisoned by a fall of broken masonry against the door. Nor do we hear that any effort was made to save them, though their cries were heard for seven days afterwards. Thus they perished slowly, many going to the place and listening to their shouts, being, as the chronicler reports,* grieved at the enormity of their crime; but none of their friends were there to help or console them : "And thus they intoxicated themselves with wine ; they went to drink wine and perished in wine."

The insurgents had proclaimed as they burst in that no robbery would be permitted. The temptation must have been very great. The whole house was full of magnificent plate, jewels, and furniture. The keeper of the wardrobe afterwards swore that he did not believe any king had a better wardrobe, or one as magnificent. Five carts, he asserted, would hardly have carried all the silver and jewels, not to mention the pure gold and gilt plate.

* Knighton.

The De-
struction
of the
Savoy.
The
accursed
thing.

But the rioters heeded nothing. They were
"zealots for truth and justice," they said, "not
thieves and robbers." It is recorded that one
of them, overcome by the beauty of a silver
goblet, took it and hid it in his bosom. But
he had been seen, and was denounced by a
comrade. Immediately the unhappy wretch
was seized, and, together with the accursed
thing which he had taken, he was cast alive
into the flames. With all this profession of
lofty aims, it is a little ludicrous to read that
they took a doublet of the Duke's, and, setting
it on a pole, shot at it with arrows, wishing the
owner was inside it.

Stow, in his *Annals*, adds to other accounts
the rumour that three barrels of gunpowder,
which the insurgents supposed to be gold or
silver, were cast into the fire, "which, more
suddenly than they thought, blew up the Hall,
destroyed the houses, and almost themselves."
Gunpowder was not in common use in those
days; but the destruction was complete enough
to warrant the report. The house seems to
have been utterly dismantled. In September 1382 the Duke sent an order to John
de Norton, "Porter de Sauvoye," to deliver the lead in his charge to Peter Clete of
Lamborne, plumber, to be employed in the
roofing of his castle at Hertford. And he

obtained from his nephew, the young King, various allowances for money lost in the burning. One of these (24th April 1382) released him from payment of "diversas summas" received both from Edward the Third and from Richard himself, making mention of the destruction of the books of account and memoranda, "in his manor of the Savoy, at the time when certain of the commons last made insurrection against our peace." And in a letter to his treasurer (20th February 1382) the Duke absolved his butler, William Overbury, for several tuns of wine which he had given away to different people and on different occasions, but especially for eighteen tuns, one pipe, and three-quarters of a pipe, of various wines destroyed by the commons, "en le temps del grant rumour."* There are other letters of this kind relating to the plate and wardrobe, but they do not add much to our information. The Savoy was totally destroyed, with its magnificent contents, and from this time until Henry VII. determined to found an hospital on the site, we have no evidence that it was anything but a ruin. Even the old walls that remained were removed by Henry VIII., and we have no reason to suppose that any part of the buildings of John of Gaunt

---

* This document gives some curious particulars of historical interest, and is printed in Appendix C.

*The De-
struction
of the
Savoy.*

have survived to our day. It is very possible,
as we have seen, that the chapel stands on the
old site, but from what we know of the plan of
the hospital, it is very unlikely that in any other
part the arrangements of the manor-house were
preserved.

RUINS OF THE BARRACK AND PRISON.

(*From a Drawing by R. Banks.*)

CHAPTER VI.

𝕿𝖍𝖊 𝕾𝖆𝖛𝖔𝖞 𝖎𝖓 𝕽𝖚𝖎𝖓𝖘.

John of Gaunt's Will—The Savoy settled on the Crown
—The List of Stewards—Extracts from their Miscel-
laneous Accounts—Savoy Street—The Hertishorne
—The Cecil Estate—The Prison—Richard Tabbe's
Pardon—The Will of Henry VII.

JOHN OF GAUNT survived the destruction of his
palace for sixteen years, during which time the
site was not wholly neglected. Esmond Hyndon
was appointed Steward in March 1382, but his
term of office was very short, for in. September
of the same year we find a warrant addressed to
John de Norton for the removal of lead for the
use of the builders at Hertford Castle. Some
lead was also sold in the following March, and
for several years the annals of the Savoy only
record the gradual dismantling and ruin of all
the buildings. At the Duke's death at Ely
Place, Holborn, 2d February 1399, he left a

The Savoy in ruins. will in which there is no mention whatever of the Savoy, though John Cokeyn is spoken of as " chief steward of my lands." He makes bequests to a great number of people, and desires his body to be buried beside that of his "most dear late wife Blanche." This was his first wife, but he founded a chantry at Leicester for the soul of the second, Constance, and made handsome provision for the third, Katherine, whose posterity, in the person of Henry VII., the son of her great-grand-daughter Margaret Beaufort, was destined more than a hundred years later to bring back the prosperity of the Savoy for a time.

The Savoy settled on the Crown. The year of Duke John's death is remarkable in our history for another event. On the 14th October, Henry of Bolingbroke, who a fortnight before had become King of England, annexed the Manor of the Savoy, with all the other estates of the house of Lancaster, to the Crown, but at the same time declared them a separate inheritance, distinct from those of the sovereign. As it is under this charter that our present gracious Queen is lady of our manor, I venture to print a summary of it in the appendix.*

The list of Stewards. Norton had been succeeded as steward or bailiff by John Ekleston in 1393, and he was succeeded in 1405 by Thomas Covell. The

* See Appendix G.

next stewards of whom we find any notice were Thomas Beaston in 1413, and Michael Craneville in 1420. Two years later we find mention of a bailiff, John Whytok; and the list down to 1509 was as follows :—William Stokes, bailiff in 1483; John Kendal, steward in 1484, afterwards prior of St. John; John Newbury, bailiff in 1485; Ralph Billington, steward in 1486; William Coope, bailiff in 1501; and John Muscot, steward in 1504.

During all this time we hear of leases being granted, of houses being built, of shops which had been burnt renewed, of gardens fenced in, of receipts for waifs, strays, forfeitures, and deodands. Some of these items are of topographical value, some are only curious. We read of boats wrecked. One entry is for "a sword, stray, not valued." Another is for a sword forfeited, for which 2od. was obtained. The garden produce was also sold. Repairs were bestowed upon the tower called "Symeon Toure," as also upon the gate toward the street and the water gate. One of these buildings was probably used as the gaol of the lord of the manor. In 1394 Thomas Shrewsbury, who was the gaoler, was fined 100s. for permitting the escape of a prisoner who had killed a man within the liberty. Between the garden and the house of the Bishop of Carlisle there was a wall called the "Mudwall." It was repaired in 1395. About the same time there is an entry for 82 lbs. of iron for a lattice for the eastern window of the tower for the safe custody of the prisoners. Of a similar character is the payment, in 1401-2 of 11s. 6d. for a pair of stocks and a ducking-stool, bought, and for a pillory, mended. Three cannons were kept in the Savoy, and occasionally paraded before the citizens, presumably at reviews. The rector of the Strand rented a house and garden for 13s. 4d. A "clerk," so described, but not of necessity a clergyman, in our sense of the word, Thomas de Lincoln, drowned himself in the Thames at the Savoy in 1401, and his goods to the amount of 60s. are forfeited. In 1482 * there is a writ to the auditor of the Duchy to allow 13s. 4d. to a tenant who had been wrongfully charged. One curious payment occurs at intervals of 6s. 8d. by way of reward "to the keper of our hows accustumed for oure counseillours of our said duchie in Powle's churche-yerde to here the worde of God there said." This entry is the more interesting when we remember the important place of the sermon at Paul's Cross, in the history of the reigns of Edward IV., of his unfortunate son, and of Richard III. One of the payments was made

* 20 *May, Reg. Edw. IV.* f. 113, b.

in the very year of Dr. Shaw's famous sermon on Wisdom, iv. 3, when the legitimacy of Edward V. was first publicly called in question.* Another entry gives us the first mention of "Savoy Strete." It relates to a house named the "Hertishorne," situated between the "Floure de lise" and the garden of the prior of St. John. It is thus probable that the prior had retained a garden by the river when he resigned his stewardship to take up the higher office. Many years later, the Fleur de lis was leased to Sir W. Cecil, and its site was long the residence of his descendants, the Earls of Exeter.

A mention of the prison is also interesting. Under the date of October 19, 1501, the Register of the time of Henry VII. (f. 179), contains a pardon to Richard Tabbe, of the parish of St. Clement Danes, without the bars of the New Temple, London, in the county of Middlesex, "gentilman, alias dicto Ricardo Tabbe custodi gaolæ sive prisonæ nostræ ducatus nostri Lancastriæ de Savoy, alias dicto Ricardo Tabbe, custodi prisonæ de Savoy," for allowing the "escapium sive evasionem" of one Robert Porter committed to his charge. Who Porter was and what he had done we know not.

The time was now approaching when the desolation was to be removed, and a gleam of

* See *Lancaster and York*, by James Gairdner, p. 208.

The Savoy in ruins.

Savoy Street.

The Hertishorne.

The Cecil Estate.

The Prison.

Richard Tabbe's pardon.

prosperity to brighten the old site. The Savoy was about to enter on the second stage of its existence. We have seen it a palace ; it was now about to become a hospital.

Henry VII., who signed Richard Tabbe's pardon at his "manor of Richmond," in Surrey, died there on Saturday, 21st April 1509. This event, by giving effect to certain provisions of his will, instilled new life into the Savoy. We have but little knowledge of its condition at the time. The garden had probably been divided. A row of new houses, each with premises extending to the water's edge, had probably been built. The ruins of the larger buildings of the manor-house no doubt remained, roofless and dilapidated ; the greater and lesser gateways and Symond's Tower probably formed the gaol ; and we have reason to believe that at least a fragment remained of the chapel, with its surrounding burial-ground.

As an important document* in our history, I must here insert a copy in full of that part of Henry's will which relates to the Savoy :—

---

* This passage is omitted from the summary of the will in the *Testamenta Vetusta.* I am, therefore, the more willing to give this copy, made by Mr. Martin for the work.

The Savoy in ruins.
The will of
Henry VII.

EXTRACT FROM THE WILL OF HENRY VII.

" And forasmuch as we inwardly consideir
that the vij. workes of Charite and Mercy bee
moost profitable, due and necessarie for the sal-
vation of man's soule, and that the same vij.
works stand moost commonly in vj. of theim ;
that is to saye in viseting the sik, mynistring
mete and drinke and clothing to the nedy,
logging of the miserable pouer, and burying of
the dede bodies of cristen people ; we therefor
gretely tendring the same, and considering that
the next way to doo and execute the said vj.
works of Pitie and Mercy, ys by meanes of
kepying, susteynyng and maynteynyng of commune Hospitallis, wherin if thei be duly kept,
the said nedie pouer people bee lodged, visited
in their siknesses, refresshed with mete and
drinke, and if nede be with clothe, and also
buried yf thei fourtune to die withine the same ;
and understanding also that there be fewe or
noon such commune Hospitallis within this our
Reame, and that for lack of theim, infinite
nombre of pouer nedie people miserably dailly
die, no man putting hande of helpe or remedie ;
We therefor of our great pitie and compassion,
desiring inwardly the remedy of the premisses,
have begoune to erecte, buylde and establisshe

a commune Hospital in our place called the *Savoie* besid Charing Crosse, nigh to our citie of London, and the same we entende with Godd's grace to finish, after the maner, fourme and fashion of a plat which is devised for the same, and signed with our hande, and have endowed with landis and tenements to the yerely value of D. marcs above all reprises, to bere maynteyne and susteign therewith, as wel oon hundreth bedds garnished, to receive and lodge nightly oon hundreth pouer folks, as also a certain nomber of Preists, and other ministers and servitours, men and women, as such a matier shall require ; to have the kepyng, rulyng and guyding of the said Hospitall and pouer folks, and ministring unto theim metes, drinks and other necessaries ; and also to doo, execute and perfourme diverse other thinges within our said Hospitall, to the laude of God the weale of our soule, and the refresshing of the said pouer people, in daily, nightly and hourely exploytyng the said vj works of Mercy, Pitie, and Charite, after suche statuts and ordenances, as we intende to make for the better ordring and directing of the said Hospitall ; and if this be nat fully and perfitely finisshed perfourmed and doon, or that the said statuts be not entierly made by our self in our life, we wol that then al the premisses and every of theim, bee doon by our executours assone as goodly may be doon after our decesse.

And for the buylding of the said Hospitall, and furst provision of cc. bedds fully garnisshed for the said c. pouer men, boks, chalices, vestments, aultre clothes, aultre tables, and other implementes necessarie for our said Hospital, the chapel of the same, and other houses of offices to the same Hospital belonging, and for the more redye payment of the money that shal be requisite for the furnisshing of the same, We have delivered in redy money before the hande, the some of ten thousand marcs, to the Dean and Chapitre of our Cathedral Church of Pawlis, within our citie of London, as by writings indented betwix us and theim, testifieng the same payment and receipt, and bering date at the —— daie of the —— moneth of —— the xxiiij. yere of our reigne, it dooth more plainly appere; the same ten thousand marcs, and every parcel therof, to be truly emploied and bestowed by suche a persone or persones, as we in our lif shal depute and appointe to be Maister of our werks, by our lettres in forme of a plakard, signed with oure hande and sealed with our signet; or if the said werks bee not doon and finisshed in our life, as our Executours after our decesse, by their writing, shall depute and assigne to be Maister of the said werks, about and upon the finisshing and perfourmyng of the said works, and for provision of the said Bedds, Books, Chalices, vestiments, aultre clothes, aultre tables, and implements, as nede shall require by the device, comptrollement and oversight of suche persons as we, or our said executours, in maner beforesaied shall depute and assigne, without discontynuyng of the said works or any parte of theim, till they bee fully perfourmed, finisshed and accomplisshed; The said ten thousand marcs to bee delivered by the said Dean and Chapitre, by bille and billes indented, to the said Maister of our said werks in our lif, and aftre in maner before said, by such parcellis and particuler somes from tyme to tyme, as the necessitie of the said works shall require, and as shal be desired and required by the said Maister of our said werks, with suche persons as shall have the controllement and oversight of the same to the intent above rehersed, by indentures to be made betwixt the said Dean and Chapitre and the said Maistre of our werks, testifieng the delivering and receipt of the said particuler somes of money; and that as wel the said Dean and his successours, for the delivere of the said particular somes to the said Maistre of our werks, by the desire and requeste beforesaied, as also the

said Maistre for th' employing and bestowing of
the said some of ten thousand marcs and every
parcel thereof, of and upon the premisses, be
accomptable to us in our life, and to our executours after our decesse, for such parcell therof,
as then shall reste not emploied ner bestowed
upon the said premesses and provision after our
deceasse, as often and whatsoever we or thei
shall calle theim therunto, as it is more largely
expressed in the said indentures. And in caas
the said x.m. marcs shall not suffice for the
hool perfourmaunce and accomplisment of the
premisses and every parcell of theim, and that
thei be not perfitely finisshed by us in our
daies ; we then wol that our executours from
tyme to tyme as necessitie shall require by like
indentures, and upon like accompte, deliver to
the said Dean and Chapitre for the tyme beyng,
as moch money above the said x.m. marcs as
shall suffice for the perfite finisshing and perfourmyng of the premisses and every parte of
theim ; the same money to be emploied and
bestowed upon the perfite finisshing and perfourmyng of the said premisses, by the said
Maistre of our werks, by the said oversight,
comptrollement and accompte, without desist-
ing or discontynuyng of the same werks in any
wise, till thei and every parcell of theim as
before is saied, bee fully and perfitely accom-

The Savoy in ruins. plisshed and perfourmed in maner and fourme afore rehersed.

And in like wise, if it be not doon by our silf, we wol that our said executours make two semblable comune Hospitallis, as wel in fourme and faction as yerely value in landis, nombre of Preists, Ministres, servants, bedds for pouer folks, and statuts and ordenances; the oon of theim to be made in some convenient place in the suburbes of our citie of York, and the other in the suburbes of our citie of Coventre, either of theim as nigh to the same cities as conveniently may be doon. And that our executours for the perfourming and fournisshing of the same, take of our said money, juelx, plate and revenues, for either of the said two Hospitallis, twenty thousand marks, which is fourty thousand marks in the hool."

CHAPTER VII.

𝕿𝖍𝖊 𝕳𝖔𝖘𝖕𝖎𝖙𝖆𝖑 𝖙𝖜𝖎𝖈𝖊 𝕱𝖔𝖚𝖓𝖉𝖊𝖉.

Delays—Boundaries—Dedication—Constitution—Seal—Completed in 1517—The First Master—The Sights of London in 1520—Unanswered Questions—The Estates—The Expenses—Suppression—Bridewell—Restoration.

The Hospital twice founded.

THE Hospital thus provided for was not actually opened for several years. A large number of legal forms had to be gone through, the site had to be cleared, the buildings erected, and the officers and inmates appointed. In 1511 (3d April) the site was conveyed to the late King's executors. In some books the whole manor itself is said to have been so conveyed. But this is an error. The site only of John of Gaunt's manor-house, part of which, as we have seen, was still in ruins, part rebuilt and used as a prison, and part laid out in a garden, was granted to the executors. The boundaries are very distinctly defined. The grant consists of

Delays.

Boundaries.

Tho Hospital twice founded.

"scitum manerii nostri de Savoy," otherwise described as of old, in the words "quondam placeam, seu peciam terræ, vocatum Le Savoy :" it is situated in the parishes of St. Clement Danes outside the bars of the New Temple, and of St. Mary "de Stronde," in the county of Middlesex, and lies between the land and mansion of the Bishop of Worcester on the east, the land of the Bishop of Carlisle on the west, abutting on the Thames at its southern, and on the high road between the Strand Cross and Charing Cross, on its northern, side. In 1512 (5th July) there is licence* to the same executors to found the hospital. The names mentioned in this charter are those of Richard (Fox), Bishop of Winchester, Lord Privy Seal; Richard (Fitz-James) Bishop of London; Thomas (Ruthall or Rowthall) Bishop of Durham; Edmund (Audley) Bishop of Salisbury; William (Smith) Bishop of Lincoln; John (Fisher) Bishop of Rochester; Thomas (Fitz Alan) Earl of Arundel; Thomas (Howard) Earl of Surrey; Sir Charles Somerset, "Lord de Herbert," chamberlain; Sir John Fyneux, Chief-Justice; Sir Robert Rede, Chief-Justice of the Common Pleas; John Yong, Master of the Rolls; Sir Thomas Lovell, Treasurer of the Household; and John Cutte, sub-treasurer of England.

* Appendix H.

This mortmain licence constitutes the hospital and prescribes that it shall consist of "five chaplains, namely, a master and four other chaplains," to the honour of our Saviour, the Blessed Virgin, and St. John the Baptist, to pray for the King, his Queen Katherine, for their souls and for the souls of Henry VII. and Elizabeth, his Queen, and of Arthur, the late Prince of Wales. It is to be called the Hospital of the late King Henry VII. of the Savoy; and is to possess a seal.

The Hospital twice founded.

Dedication.

Impressions of this seal have been repeatedly engraved.* It represents St. John the Baptist holding the Lamb and the flag. On the right is a portcullis and on the left a rose with a stalk and leaves.

Seal

The buildings must have been well advanced by 1514, for on the 25th November in that year, Wolsey, now Archbishop of York, held a council at the Savoy, and three days later, 28th November, another. We know the builder's name. He was Humphrey Cook, carpenter to the King, and dying in 1530, was buried here.

In 1516 (4th July) there is a letter from Pope Leo X. to Wolsey asking him to obtain from the King the payment of certain moneys due to Aloysius Gibraleon, who is described as

* *Archæologia*, vol. xix. p. 146.

The Hospi-
tal twice
founded.

Completed
in 1517.

The first
Master.

"cubicularius," and as writer of apostolic letters, for transmitting the plenary indulgence for "the hospital of the poor in the suburbs of the city of London in the place called Savoy."

In March of the following year (1517) the Hospital may be said to have been opened. The executors of Henry VII. in a deed, of which several copies exist,* recite the patent or charter of 1511, and its confirmation in 1512, and proceed to found the hospital with its chaplains, in order that they may fulfil the duties named above, in praying for the souls of the King and his family, in performing divine service, giving alms, doing other works of piety and mercy, succouring the poor, visiting the sick, giving food to the hungry, drink to the thirsty, clothes to the naked, and burial to the dead.

They then name William Holgill, priest, who had superintended the building, to be the first Master, and invest him with all the temporalities and spiritualities of the office.

Next they appoint John Sutton, "in decretis licentiatum," to be sub-master; Thomas Thornegh, priest, to be sacristan; Alexander Palmer, Bachelor of Divinity, to be confessor; and Christopher Harebotell, priest, to be hospitaller. These four, with William Holgill, were to form the Chaplains of the Hospital, to have a common

* *Add. MSS.*, 11599; *Lansdowne MSS.*, 651, etc.

seal; and to have power as a corporate body to plead in all courts; to hold the lands and perform all other functions as owners, in "frank almoigne," of the site of the manor of the Savoy.

There is something very vague in this and the other documents relating to the objects of the new foundation. It seems literally to have been something like a monastery with a limited number of brethren, and to have been instituted, as we may reasonably suppose, chiefly for the purpose of making continual prayer for the souls of the founder and his kin. The enormous development of the doctrine of purgatory, including that of indulgences, in the years immediately preceding the Reformation, must be held accountable for this and many similar foundations.

The buildings erected on the site of the old palace must have been of great magnificence. Of them all, only the chapel now remains. The last remnants of the other buildings, used as a storehouse, were on the south-west side of the church, and extended to the water's edge, until the Victoria Embankment was made. Last year (1877) even this fragment was removed.

Our frontispiece represents the last charred fragments of the eastern portion before they were overwhelmed by the approaches to Waterloo

*The Hospi-
tal twice
founded.*

The sights
of London
in 1520.

Bridge.   The view was taken early in the present century.*

That the new buildings were considered among the sights of London we may gather from the following curious notes which Mr. Martin has extracted from a manuscript in the British Museum.†   The Lords of the Council write to Wolsey on the 2d July 1520 that his letters of the 26th June, informing them of the coming hither of three French gentlemen, were received on Thursday last.   The gentlemen themselves arrived the same evening suddenly in London.   " Though we had short warning, convenient preparations were made according to your pleasure.   The Mayor of London made unto them, being well accompanied with gentlemen of England, a goodly banquet at night in Chepesyde, and there they saw the watch, which was right well ordered, and by them excellently commended.   The next day after, being St. Peter's day, we sent the Lord Barnes (Berners) to give welcomings to the said gentlemen, and to accompany them.   And the same day the said Mayor had them [to] dinner, and in the afternoon, inasmuch as they desired among other things to see

* Eighteen impressions of this print were taken off as proofs before letters, and may be had from Mrs. Noseda in the Precinct (109 Strand).
† Calig. D. vii. 233.

the *Hospital of Savoy* and the King's Chapel at
the monastery of Westminster, they were conveyed thither, well accompanied on horseback,
and . . . demonstrations made unto them of
notable th[ings in] the said hospital, the King's
Chapel and the sa[id monastery]. The Abbot
of the same accompanying them t . . . .
entertained them with right goodly cheer, [as . .
the . . u]sage required upon a Friday. And on
S[aturday] following one of the sheriffs gave them
a goodly dinner, and the tide being commodious,
they went to Richmond about noon with Lords
Barnes, Darcy, and others, where they visited
the Princess Mary. Her chamber was well
furnished and attended by goodly gentlemen
and tall yeomen, and ladies, the Duchess of
Norfolk and others. The Princess entertained
the French gentlemen with goodly countenance
and playing on the virginals, at which they
marvelled considering her tender age. . . . . .
Strawberries, wine, wafers, and ypocras in
plenty. The same night the other sheriff gave
them a goodly supper. On Sunday the Duke of
Norfolk entertained them. To-day they will see
the Tower, and leave." W[estm.] 2 July, signed
by the Duke of Norfolk, the Bishop of Winchester, the Bishop of Lincoln, Lord Berners,
John Abbot [of Westm.] Robert Brudenell,
John Fyneux, T. Wyndam, and others.

The Hospital twice founded.

In January of the year 1524 the statutes were confirmed, and from them we hear of the appointment of two priests, no doubt as assistants; of a matron and women under her, of a medical man and a surgeon, a bread maker, a cook and sub-cook, a gardener, and a porter; and of the reception of the poor and sick, and the provision of a hundred beds. Over the principal entrance was this inscription on a tablet :*—" 1505. Hospitium hoc inopi turbe Savoia vocatum Septimus Henricus fundavit ab imo solo."

It would thus appear that even though in the religious changes of the next few years the duties of the Master and Chaplains ceased so far as the special prayers were concerned, plenty of work of another kind was provided for them. In 1535 a commission was issued to inquire into the state of the Hospital. Unfortunately we have only the questions asked and not the answers to them. They are as follows :—

Unanswered Questions.

" ARTICLES OF INQUISICION TOUCHING THE SAVOYE."

" 1. Firste whether there be iiij. chaplains beside the Mr. in this house according to the fundacion, et nominentur.

* *Vetusta Monumenta*, vol. ii., where see also several prints and plans of the Hospital.

2. Item. Whether there be ij. conductes preestes ; ij. honest secular men that be lettred, wherof thone is subsexten, thother sub-hospitalar ; foure honest men called altaristes ; and other v. servauntes, viz. a clerke of the kechyn, a panter, a coke, a gardener, and a porter ; and ij. other servauntes wherof thone to be underporter and thother underporter. And also one matrone and under her xij. other honest women in this house, according to the said fundacion.

3. Item. Whether the Mr. of this house doe kepe any moo than ij. servauntes to wayte upon hym on the charges of this house.

4. Item. What benefices and howe many hath the Mr. of this house besides this ; and howe many he received or atteigned sen he was Mr. here.

5. Item. Whether he have any office or service of or undre any other person besides this house.

6. Item. How long hath he ben absent at one or sundrie tymes in any yere from this house sen he was ; and about what busynes he hath ben so absent.

7. Item. Yf he say that he hath moo benefices, and that he was absent, what dispensations or licences he hath so to doo.

8. Item. Whether the Mr. do ij. in a weke at the leste see the poore men lett in, and over-

see his ministers diligently whether they doo
their office and duetie about theym.

9. Item. Whether that he provides a phisi-
cion and surgion for theym that be sik
according to the founder's will. And whether
they doo visite theym that be sik twyes every
daie according to the fundacion.

10. Item. Whether he be mercifull, beningne
and lovyng to the poore ; and not skoymys or
lothesome to visite theym or to be among
theym.

11. Item. Whether he or his ministers by
his sufferance do take in suche as they reken
moste clene of the poore, and repell theym that
they reken most sore or deseased, for avoydyng
of their owne lothesomenes or contagion.

12. Item. Whether he geve a rekenyng
yerely at ij. tymes appoynted to the iiij. chaplains of the state of the house and his admistra-
cion.

13. Item. Whether he hath solde any wood
or grove, or sett any ferme without the consent
of the said chaplains.

14. Item. Whether he hath lett out any
ferme of this house for any terme above vij.
yeres by any meane.

15 Item. Whether the worde of God be
preched here, and howe ofte in the yere.

16. Item. Whether the cth beddes, ap-

poynted by the founder be well and clenely kept and repayred, and all necessaries to theym belongyng.

17. Item. Whether any poore man do lie in any shetes unwasshed that any other lay in bifore.

18. Item. Whether they laye moo than one in a bedde.

19. Item. Whether the bathes limitted by the founder be well observed and applyed.

20. Item. Whether the Mr. of this house be or hath ben at any tyme sen he was Mr. of this house, suspected, noted or convicte of incontinence, whan, and with home.

21. Item. Whether the Mr. Chaplains and other ministers of this house be sworne to the foundacion according to the same.

Touching the Chaplains and other Ministers of the Savoye.

1. Firste. Whether they be obedient in all thinges to the Master according to the fundacion.

2. Item. Whether any of theym have any benefice with cure or otherwise, incompatible, besides this house.

3. Item. Whether any of theym hath bene absent from this house sen he was made chaplain; howe long and for what cause.

4. Item. Whether the sacriste do see all vestimentes and ornamentes apperteynyng to the church well kept and ordred and doo geve a rekenyng therof yerely according to the fundacion.

5. Item. Whether he have an inventarie therof, et eam exhibeat.

6. Whether the confessour do his duetie in visiting the poore and comforting them spirituallie.

7. Item. Whether the ij. chaplains under hym, one betwene vij. and viij. in the mornyng, and thother betwene v. and vj. in the evenyght, doo visite all the poore, and see that none of theym lack the sacramentes or other goostely comforte.

8. Item. Whether the Hospitalar and sub-hospitalar doo their duetie in ministracion of the poore, without carnall affection or partialitie, according to the fundacion.

9. Item. Whether the stuarde or vitzmaster doo his duetie in his office, and geve a rekenyng of his administracion yerely before the master and chaplains, according to the statutes.

10. Item. Whether any of theym hath ben at any tyme diffamed, suspected or convicte of felonye, or any notable cryme.

11. Item. Whether any of theym be a fighter, a sedicious person, a dronkard, a commen

haunter of taverne or alehouses, or a dicer, carder, or walker abrode by night.

12. Item. Whether the sub-hospitalar or any other minister of the poore folke doo take any money, bribes or rewardes of theym for admitting of theym to this house and lodging.

13. Item. Whether any of the susters doo cherish theym moste that hath any money, and causeth theym to spende the same whan they be within, at good ale or otherwise whereby the same might have any pleasure or prouffit theymselff.

14. Item. Whether any of the susters hath ben at any time sen their entrie to this house diffamed, suspected or convicte of any notable crime.

15. Item. Whether any of the suster be commonly dronke, sedicious, irefull, or walking foorth to the towne or elswher without good cause.

16. Item. Whether any of theym be slack or lothsome to visit the poore, to wasshe their geare or to do anything about theym that is requisite.

17. Item. Whether the Paneter, Butler, Coke, Undercoke, Gardner, Porter and Underporter doo their offices accordingly.

CIRCA STATUM DOMUS.

First. What tresure and store they have to supplie all necessities and chaunces that maye be incident to the house.

Item. Whether the buyldinges, tenementes and landes belonging to this house be well and conveniently kept and repayred.

Item. What benefices be of the guyfte or disposicion of the Master of this house.

Item. What pilgremage is here used and what prouffittes comes to this house therby.

The Estates

These questions, even without answers, give us an adequate idea of the duties demanded by the King from the Master and his associates. How the expenses connected with so great an establishment were met we may gather from two subsequent documents. The first is that portion of the *Valor Ecclesiasticus* which relates to the Savoy. From it we learn that in 1535 the Hospital was endowed with the site on which it stood, its gardens and orchards, and with "divers houses within the precinct :" various rents in London and the suburbs, at Shoreditch, Hackney, Enfield, and other places in Middlesex, amounting in all to £201 : 7 : 8, together with the offerings in the church of the Hospital amounting to £1 : 0 : 0. In Essex there were rents amounting to £117 : 2 : 8 ; in Hertfordshire to £24 : 0 : 6; in Buckinghamshire to £33 : 1 : 7½; in Cambridgeshire to £80 : 14 : 7¼; in Kent to £36 : 19 : 5½; in Derbyshire to £38 : 0 : 0; in Yorkshire to £31 : 6 : 8. The whole income, after deducting various expenses, tithes, and other outgoings of the kind, amounted to £529 : 15 : 7¾.

In the same document we have a list of the expenses of the Hospital, which were as follows :

"The Master of the Hospital asks allowance by the foundation for £158 : 3 : 4, viz. :—

	£		
The Stipend of four chaplains £4 each	£16	0	0
Two 'capellani conducti,' 66s. 8d. each	6	13	4
Officers and Servants :—			
Sub-sacrist	2	13	4
Sub-hospitaller . . .	1	6	8
Four Altarists, 26s. 8d. each .	5	6	8
Thirteen Sisters, 4s. each . .	2	12	0
Servants of the Hospital . .	18	0	0
Their livery	17	16	10
Wax, bread, and wine, for the church of the Hospital . .	6	3	10
Expenses of the poor and infirm, mending of vessels, 140 ells of canvas for burying poor, candles for the poor, payments to apothecaries for medicine."	32	1	8

The Hospital twice founded. It would thus appear that the Master and his chaplains were at least endeavouring to do their duty by the sick and suffering.

We have no complete list of the Masters, and cannot tell whether Holgill was succeeded at once by John Ellys, appointed in or about 1549. There was immediately a contest between the King's ministers and the hospital about first-fruits, which was compromised in December of the same year, the Master and Brethren agreeing to pay the large sum of £240, but being obliged to mortgage the manor of Dengey in Essex to Sir William Petre for five years in order to raise it. The Master Ellys's death happened soon after, and though the exact date is unknown, we find 109 shillings and 5 pence charged for his funeral expenses under the year 1551. A Richard Ellys, " Hospitalarius," buried in 1550, cannot have been the same. At this time the expenses of the Hospital were reported to exceed the revenue by £205 : 4 : 2, and 8339 poor or sick persons were said to have been relieved, assisted, or lodged, during the twelve months preceding September of that year.

There seems to have been some hesitation in appointing a successor to Ellys: and two curious letters on the subject written by Petre to Cecil are still extant. The first, dated 9th

September, asks Cecil's interest for the bearer, though the writer confesses to knowing nothing about him, except that he had been chosen to be master "according to the order of their foundation," and apparently is unacquainted even with his name. Both Cecil and Petre were interested in the Hospital, Cecil because of its near neighbourhood to his own holding in the Strand, of which mention has already been made, and Petre from being mortgagee of the Essex manor above mentioned. On the 14th September he wrote again, and as his letter is a curious example of the canting style of the time, I subjoin it :—*

"After my most hearty commendations, I thank you for your letters, and also for your pains for the Savoy. I doubt not but there be (as you write) good or rather great plenty of anglers for it; if they do angle for the good continuance of the poor men and of the house, I like their angling well, and whosoever hath most desire to do so, I would he might take the fish. Marry, I would all things were done in order, and every man called to such places specially rather of other men's vocation, than of their own labour. At the beginning the apostles left their fishing of fishes and became fishers of men, and now we which talk much of Christ

* *State Papers, Domestic, Edw. VI.* vol. xiii. 43.

The Hospital twice founded.

and his Holy Word have, I fear me, used a much contrary way, for we leave fishing for men and fish again in the tempestuous sees of this world for gain and wicked mammon. Thus you see lying here alone I am waxen a preacher. I do send you herewith a note of a commission for the visitation of the Savoy. W. Say was not in London, and therefore I did it myself. Ye may put out as you think good. I have put a clause that the Commissioners may reform things, which I did for that when they shall know my lord's pleasures they may do the same after their advertisement without any new commission." The applicant was Sir Robert Bowes, and his name is sometimes reckoned in the list of the masters, but probably in error.

Suppression.

The commission to which he refers was shortly afterwards issued, Sir Roger Cholmeley, Lord Chief Baron of the Exchequer, being appointed visitor. The questions to be answered were so nearly the same as those of 1535, that I need not take up space in repeating them. Sir Roger reported both on the actual state of the hospital and on the revenues. His report seems to have been taken as unfavourable ; for though Ralph Jackson, the vice-master, was appointed master on the 9th June 1553, he was required immediately to surrender the hospital to the King, who on the 26th of the same

month made over the estates, with "the implements and utensils," to the new hospital of
Bridewell, which the Lord Mayor and citizens
had founded with the royal assistance.

A special exception is made of the chapel bell,
one chalice "pro administranda communione,"
and certain other articles, not specified, necessary for divine service in the said chapel, and
for the administration of the said sacrament.
We shall have occasion to mention this exception in our account of the chapel.

Ralph Jackson's surrender is dated 10th
June 1553, the day after his appointment.
According to the accounts given by Stow,
Speed, and Heylin, the King sent for him and
his brethren, "and dealt so powerfully and
effectually with them that they presently resigned;" but this anecdote hardly tallies with
the incontestable evidence of the original documents just cited. Jackson was appointed a
prebendary of Canterbury on the 21st November 1554, occupying the stall of Thomas
Willoughby, deprived by Queen Mary, a stall
which, in the present century, has been filled by
William, first Earl Nelson, the great admiral's
brother, and in our own day by Arthur Penrhyn
Stanley, now Dean of Westminster.

The history of the Hospital does not, however,
end here. Queen Mary determined to restore

it, and probably found the buildings so far in good repair, after three years' vacancy, that there was no impediment in the way, except the want of estates for a new endowment.

The Queen's warrant was dated on 15th June 1556, being headed with the words, "By the Kinge and Queene." She recites the original purpose of the foundation, "to pray for the states and soules of sondry our progenytours kinges and quenes of this our realme," and proceeds to restore "Sir Raffe Jackson, clerk," to the office of Master, appointing with him the reduced number of three chaplains, instead of the four in the former endowment. For estates, the Queen grants the site itself, as before; the manor of Dengey in Essex, which had probably not been surrendered either to King Edward or to Bridewell, owing to Sir William Petre's mortgage, and any estates of any dissolved monastery concealed from Henry VIII. or Edward VI. which should be surrendered within twelve months, to the value of one hundred pounds a year.

On the 3d November in the same year a second warrant was issued by which *four* chaplains, as heretofore, with the Master, were appointed, namely, besides Jackson, William Mason, Thomas Stillebanckes, William Neale, and Robert Burye. A week later several small holdings, not fewer in number than thirty-four, scattered all over England, were assigned to the Hospital. In May 1558, in consideration of the surrender of these holdings, there is a fresh grant of lands, chiefly in Yorkshire and Lincolnshire, but apparently of very moderate value. They were, for the most part, in the shape of reversions which had come into the power of the Crown on the suppression of the chauntries, and being already leased, were not immediately an available source of income. This accounts for the gradual deterioration during the next 150 years of the Hospital estates, for the masters, holding only reversions, probably mortgaged them for ready money, and in many cases lost them altogether. One such arrangement was made in 1559, and others might be cited ; the Master and brethren leasing to Richard Perwick and Edward Cosen for 200 years, in consideration of a payment of £300, all their lands in Yorkshire, Middlesex, Lancashire, and Westmoreland, "at the old accustomed rents" which are not more distinctly specified. We shall, however, have occasion to return to this subject.

Some of the chroniclers relate that, the beds having all been taken away to Bridewell, the ladies of the Court, "for the better attaining of the Queen's good grace," furnished the restored

Hospital in a very ample manner. I have found no contemporary proof of this statement, but it is not in itself improbable. Dean Feckenham gave the chapel some "verie fayre plate," and a chalice with a cover double gilt.

In December 1557 Ralph Jackson, Master of the Savoy, was appointed to the Rectory of St. Clement Danes, and was succeeded, it would seem, by Edward Thurland, of whose appointment I find no record.* On the 17th November 1558 Queen Mary died.

I may note, in concluding this chapter, that in 1552 the first English glass-factory is said to have been established in the Savoy. It is hardly needful to say that in times much earlier than these glass had been made in England. Of the Savoy factory little else seems to have been recorded. There is still a glass-maker in the precinct, but I cannot undertake to establish any connection between the new and the old manufacture.

---

* Mr. Gwynne, in his interesting paper in the *Church Chronicle*, July 1869, mentions "Mr. Absolon, Master," appointed in 1559 or 1560. His authority is a MS. history by John Wilkinson, of whom I have much to say farther on. The name of Absolon does not, however, occur in any other or contemporary records to which I have had access. The same authority postpones Thurland's appointment to 16th July 1561.

CHAPTER VIII.

The Hospital under Queen Elizabeth.

THE accession of Queen Elizabeth found the Savoy Hospital in existence, but that was all. We hear no more of thousands of poor and sick relieved, no more of the seven works of mercy, no more of solemn services. At first there seems to have been some idea of suppressing it a second time, but it escaped, as much perhaps because of its insignificance as for any other reason. There were no longer large estates to be obtained by some rapacious noble. The buildings were not suited to the requirements of a great household. The new

*The Hospi-
tal under
Queen
Elizabeth.*

Thurland's
schemes.

Master, Thurland, was too busy with schemes
of a different kind to bring the Savoy into
prominence for its charities, or for any other
reason. We find him surrounded by a number
of men of the class immortalised by Scott
under the name of Dousterswivel. They seem
to have been countrymen of that famous German, and persuaded Thurland that great wealth

was to be obtained by working certain mines in
Cumberland, where some estates, perhaps those
of the Hospital, were situated. As early as
1561 he is in conference with one of these
adventurers, John Steynbergh; again, it is with
Hans Lonar, or Daniel Ulsteyd. Next it is
with Daniel Hochstetter, who seems to have
accompanied him to Keswick, where many
attempts were made to find ores worth digging
up. Specimens were forwarded to Cecil, the
Secretary of State, and being assayed were found
wanting. This was in March 1565. In April
some allowance was made to the adventurers in
consideration of the commencement of operations. In May they found copper containing
silver, and desired a warrant from the Queen to
let them bring over three or four hundred foreign
workmen. In July they were allowed to cut
wood for the works, and at the same time were
directed to apprehend certain disorderly characters employed by them.

The only possible end to this kind of ignorant speculation arrived very soon. At the close of the month last mentioned, Thurland was arrested for debt, although, in a letter announcing the fact, he sends Cecil a specimen of ore from Borrowdale. A month later he proposes a composition with his creditors, which seems to have caused a delay in his mining operations, yet in May 1566 he is again writing to Cecil, announcing that gold and silver are to be found at Keswick, but that the secret is well kept, and begging for some skilful workmen out of Flanders. There are many similar letters. Operations, always promising, seem never to have brought in any money, and were always more expensive than he expected. Finally, in September 1566, he is so much in debt that he must keep to the house, and writes praying for protection from his creditors for a few years. He has pawned plate, probably that of the Savoy, but this does not plainly appear, and wants the Queen to take up the pledges. So he goes on always finding something valuable, but without any distinct result, till the Earl of Northumberland interposes, refusing to allow the ore to be carried away, and declaring the miners trespassers. This obstacle seems to have been surmounted, probably by the influence of Cecil, and for a short time things seem to go better, but in 1568 he declares himself ruined, and begs leave to go abroad if some relief cannot be afforded.

Meanwhile, how has the Hospital fared ? In 1566 Gabriel Goodman, at that time Dean of Westminster, writes to Cecil, warning him that the estates were likely to be injured by some dealings between the Master and a Mr. Fanshawe. The Dean excuses himself for interfering, not being himself Visitor, yet feeling " in conscience bounde to that poore Hospitall." Perhaps it was in consequence of this letter that the Bishop's attention was called to the state of the house, and in 1569, the lease which I described in the last chapter, to Richard Perwick and Edward Cosens, was called in question. At first it was thought to be a forgery, but later was believed to have been granted by the Master without the knowledge of his brethren. It was also alleged that Thurland had placed the Hospital in debt to one Curteys, a pewterer, for £200, had received to his own use as much as 1000 marks, had kept his kinsfolk to the number of five in his lodgings, and had neglected to reside himself, had not seen to the poor, nor looked to the gate, as bound by the statute to do.

One of those characteristic papers of Cecil's, a kind of catechism which he put to himself, exists as to the Savoy at this time, and is worth quoting in full :—*

" THE OBJECTIONS MADE AGAINST THE BILL OF THE SAVOYE, AND ANSWERS THEREUNTO.

" 1. The bill establisheth the erection and foundation made by the executors of King Henry VII., and every article and thing therein contained. In which foundation is contained matter of superstition and idolatry, as saying of mass, praying for the dead, etc., not meet to be allowed.

" 2. The bill reciteth that Thurland made divers leases without the consent of the chaplains : the provision of the bill is that leases made by Thurland and the chaplains above twenty-one years, etc., shall be void. So the provision is further than the cause of complaint.

" 3. The bill mentioneth four unreasonable leases as causes of complaint. The proviso extendeth to them and to all others.

" 4. The bill allegeth that Thurland, for ·the making of these leases and divers bonds, was duly convicted and deprived, which we find not proved.

" 5. By this bill the first leases should be made

* *Lansdowne MS.*, 20, fol. 48.

void, and after the "leasees" should sue for remedy in equity, which is an hard course.

"6. There be words in the bill that seem to make void not only leases made by Thurland, but also all other leases, in the sentence, *And that all give, etc.,* a little before these words, *Provided nevertheless.*

"7. It is doubtful in the proviso whether it be meant that the complaint of the leasees shall be within a year, or the same be a time limited to the commissioners, the words *within one year,* as they may be pointed, may make the sense either one way or other. And it were hard to make the authority of the commissioners to cease within a year.

"8. It is not proved that the bonds and obligations mentioned were made for Thurland's own debts.

"9. Neither are the creditors nor all the leasees here to be heard, and in their absence, without hearing what they could say, it is unmeet to proceed against them."

"ANSWERS.

"1. To the first it may be amended by inserting these words :—*Not being contrary or repugnant to the laws for religion established and now in force within this realm.*

"2. To the second, our complaint reacheth

further, for that we complain of the seal being in his own custody, and we could not in our bill complain particularly of all his actions; partly for that we know not all, and partly lest our bill should be tedious, and therefore named only the chiefest that we know.

" 3. To the third, our bill extendeth not to all other leases by Thurland demised, but to those only which are above twenty-one years, and whereof the old rent hath not been reserved, or which have not been usually demised by the space of twenty years before, wherein, notwithstanding, we refer ourselves to the discretion of the house.

" 4. To the fourth, the sentence of deprivation then read, plainly setteth down the causes, and the copy of the visitation the particulars.

" 5. To the fifth, touching the form of avoiding of them we refer ourselves to their honourable considerations.

" 6. To the sixth, our intention was that the bill should extend only to Thurland's actions, and to avoid all fines made by his leasees to the prejudice of the House; if the words reach any further in the opinion of the learned in the law, we refer ourselves to their correction. But we suppose the cause of this seeming is the error by mistaking *leasers* for *leasees*, which fault was the writer's.

" 7. To the seventh, we refer the limitation of the time given to the commissioners to your good pleasures.

" 8. To the eighth, the particulars shall be proved by the copy of the visitation, and by his own hand, which we offered to do at the last meeting of the committees, if they would have stayed to hear our proofs.

" 9. To the ninth. For remedy thereof are the commissioners appointed in the proviso."

Endorsed.—The " objections made against the bill of the Savoy and the answers thereunto."

Thurland deprived.

In July 1570, at the request of Grindall, Goodman, and another clergyman, Cecil was moved to do something. He seems to have excused Thurland, but the three writers reply, " Iff Mr. Thurland have deserved well of the commenweale (as ye seme to signyfie by your lettres) it were good reason he should be recompensed *ex publico* and not *ex sanguine pauperum.*" This letter was written on the 7th. On the 29th sentence of deprivation was pronounced against Thurland. By a memorandum sent to Cecil, it appears that he had contrived to raise no less than £2728 : 11 : 7½, out of Savoy lands, all of which he seems to have frittered away. There were many other charges against him, and some at least seem to have been but too well founded. The day after the sentence was pronounced Grindall wrote as follows to Cecil :—

EDWARD GRINDALL, ARCHBISHOP OF YORK, TO SIR WILLIAM CECIL.

" Sir, yesterdaie afternone we sate at the Savoye and fownde the Master there more untowarde to resigne then the daie before, wherefore seynge him so wilfull we proceded to sentence of deprivacion. And yet neverthelesse made a decree withall (whereof the said Master was not privy) that yf her Matie wolde under her signe manuell or seale declare a mislikinge thereof within xxx^tie dayes, that then the said sentence should be as unpronounced. He made a fond protestacion to appeale but there are no judges havinge learninge which can by lawe or justice reverse our sentence, being pronownced upon so good growndes and consideracions, and the same either confessed by himselfe or proved by sufficient witnesses. I sende you herewith the coppie of the sentence, which yf it please the Quene's Matie to reade over, I thinke her pitifull harte will muche lamente the greate abuse of her most noble grandfather's godlie foundation. We required of the saide Master Thurlande a bonde with

The Hospital under Queen Elizabeth.

one suertie, his owne bonde beinge nothinge worthe, for restitucion of so muche as shulde be dewlie proved hereafter that he had defrawded the poore howse. His awnswere was he coulde finde no suerties. We tolde him, to put him in some terror, that we had auctoritie, if we sawe cause, to committ him to warde; although in deade we never purposed so to doo, but in the ende to have taken his owne bonde. But the said Master Thurlande sodenlye withdrewe himselfe, and when we called for him againe, woorde was brought us that he was gone towardes the Courte. So we conjectured that the mention of imprisonment put him in feare which in good faithe was never mente. For I knewe to muche of her Ma^{tie's} pleasure in that behalf to deale so inconsiderately. Thus havinge made a trewe rehersall of our procedinges to meete with all contrarye reportes, I cease further to troble you and commende you to the grace of God. From the deane of Powlles howse in London, this xxx^{th} of Julye 1570.

> (*Signed*)   " Yours in Christe,
>
> " EDM. EBOR."

P.S. in the Archbishop's hand.—" After the writynge heroff, I was advertised that Mr. Thurlande went nott to the Courte, butt remayneth stille att his lodginge in the Savoye."

The Savoy was not yet rid of its wasteful master. No one was appointed in his stead, and three years elapsed without anything being done in the matter. Then Thurland took courage, and claimed to be still Master. The chaplains wrote in a fright to Cecil, now become Lord Burleigh, but their remonstrances, though urgently repeated, were of no avail. After another year's delay Thurland was reappointed, April 26, 1574.

The Hospital under Queen Elizabeth. An interregnum.

Thurland restored.

What were Burleigh's reasons for this step are not clearly known. Possibly he considered Thurland's public services, and had no great consideration for the objects of the hospital.

A curious paper (*Lansdowne MS.* 20, f. 73) throws some light on the condition of the place at this time. The substance of it is as follows :—

SAVOY. OFFICE OF THE RECEIVER-GENERAL, 15 ELIZABETH. ARREARS DUE FROM DIVERS PERSONS.

Condition of the Savoy.

From Sir Ralph Sadler, chancellor of the duchy of Lancaster, occupier of certain houses and chambers called "Le Duchie Lodginge," £10 per annum. For three years to Mich. 15 Eliz., £30.

N.B.—Will. Cade, Receiver of the Queen, used to pay this.

From William Savile, gent., part of the rent of certain lands in Sowthrey, 45s. 8d. per annum. For three years to the Annunciation, 14 Eliz., £7 : 19 : 10.

From Edward Earl of Oxford, part rent of two tenements within the Hospital, late in the tenure of John Hurleston, £4, and Barnard Hampton, 63s. 4d. £10 : 11 : 8.

From Thos. Haines, Esq., half the rent of a chamber, 13s. 4d.

From Dorothea Brodbelt, lady of the Privy Chamber, for rent of a chamber at 1lb. of pepper a year, unpaid for ten years. 10lbs. of pepper.

From Adam Purselow for the manor of Hooton, Yorks, £10 : 19 : 5.

From Sir Henry Lee,* half the rent of certain chambers in the Hospital. £3 : 6 : 8.

From Ralph Bowes, gent., half the rent of a tenement. 10s.

From Richard Thomew, Esq., executor of the will of Mary Finche, lady of Queen Mary's Privy Chamber, for a legacy due to the Hospital, left this fifteenth year. £3 : 6 : 8.

* The Rev. F. G. Lee, D.C.L., has kindly shown me some papers relating to this tenant, his ancestor.

Endorsed by Burleigh.—" Savoye Arrerages of rentes due at Mich. 15°."

The rules imposed on Thurland by Burleigh, as the conditions of his restoration, are in the same collection. He was enjoined to reside at least six months of the year, to resort to divine service every Sunday and holy day at the least, to dine with the chaplains and come to table in good time, to avoid meddling with the receipts of the Hospital, to consent that the salary of the master during the four years of his deprivation should be applied to the payment of the money he had lost, together with £5 a year deducted from his income. All this and more he very solemnly swore to perform, and Lord Burleigh in addition gave him some very good advice as to his outward behaviour for the avoiding of scandal, all which he promised to follow.

At this time the revenues of the Hospital were only £254 : 6 : 8 a year, and the expenses very much greater.

When or how Thurland died we do not know. The point is hardly worth the trouble of clearing up, though it would be interesting to learn if he reformed in his last years. His successor, of whom we know little but his name, was Doctor Mount, and the date of his appointment may have been in 1575 or 1577. There are State papers, dated in both those years, relating to the

The Hospital under Queen Elizabeth.

Thurland's promises of reformation.

Thurland's successor, Dr. Mount.

condition and revenues of the Hospital, which may have been drawn up on the vacancy. It was during Dr. Mount's incumbency that the abortive rising of the Earl of Essex took place, and troops were stationed in the Savoy apparently to protect Lord Burleigh, whose house, as

we have seen, was opposite. This is the first time the hospital buildings were used as a barrack, but by no means the last. Dr. Mount died apparently in 1602, and was succeeded by Dr. Neale, who in 1605 became Dean of Westminster, vacating the mastership of the Savoy. He had been domestic chaplain to Lord Burleigh, but of his incumbency here I know nothing further. On the 24th March 1603 Queen Elizabeth died at Richmond.

THE SAVOY HOSPITAL IN 1650.

(Reduced from a Print by G. Vertue.)

CHAPTER IX.

𝕿𝖍𝖊 𝕳𝖔𝖘𝖕𝖎𝖙𝖆𝖑 𝖚𝖓𝖉𝖊𝖗 𝖙𝖍𝖊 𝕾𝖙𝖊𝖜𝖆𝖗𝖙𝖘.

Lodgers in the Savoy—Lord Carew—Lord Northampton
—Bishop Montaigne's Successor—Walter Balcanquall—The Archbishop of Spalato.

RICHARD NEALE became Dean of Westminster
in 1605. He was succeeded at the Savoy after
some delay by George Montaigne or Mountain,
appointed on the 22d October 1608. It is
possible that Dr. Neale did not resign the Savoy
on first going to Westminster, but held it until
he obtained the bishopric of Rochester in
October 1608. He held his Deanery with the
Bishopric till his translation to Lichfield in 1610.

Dr. Montaigne did not remain long at the
Savoy. On his predecessor's appointment to
Lichfield he succeeded him at Westminster.
His incumbency is only marked by a little paper
entitled, "An accompt of George Montaigne,
Doctor in Divinitie and Maister of the Hos-

pitall of the Savoy . . . . . . for one whole
year." After reading this document we can
guess at a secret which might otherwise have
presented a difficulty. How was it that a
number of eminent divines were willing to
accept a piece of preferment which, according to
the last accounts, was practically unendowed?

We must remember that in the early years of
the Stewart dynasty the most fashionable street
in London was the Strand. From Lord
Arundel's palace near Temple Bar to Lord
Suffolk's new house at Charing Cross, there
was an almost unbroken line of the mansions
of the great nobility. Thomas, second Lord
Burleigh, created Earl of Exeter in 1605, lived
in his father's house, where now is Exeter Hall.
His garden is now Burleigh Street. Opposite,
where we have Salisbury and Cecil Streets, his
half-brother, Robert, who had become Earl of
Salisbury in 1605, had his town house. Not
far off were Lord Southampton's and Lord
Buckingham's, both commemorated in modern
streets. On the other side of the Savoy was
Somerset House, where the Queen, Anne of
Denmark, kept her Court. It may be easily
understood without further explanation, that the
Savoy stood in the very centre of the most
fashionable quarter of London, and the master,
in default of more regular sources of income,

used to let chambers to such noblemen and gentlemen as could afford high rents for the sake of lodging there.

This is the "accompt" for one whole year, so far as it relates to "Tenements within the Savoy gates":—

"The innermost tower near the chapel door with other rooms, Sir David Murrye's lodgings by lease for yeares, rent a year, £4.

The great Tower or Gatehouse, Lord Carowe's lodgings by lease, rent £6.

Sir Robert Dormer's lodging, rent £4.

Lord Compton's lodging, £4.

Lord Mordaunt's lodging, £9.

Countess of Exeter's lodging, now in possession of Mr. John Dackomb, £2.

Sir George Manner's lodging, by the Common Water Gate, £1.

Mr. Brigham's lodging, 4s.

Mr. Roger Manner's lodging, now Sir Francis Fane's, over the Poor Gate, £1.

Mr. Warewood's lodging, now Lord Carowe's, £1.

Total £32 : 4 : 8."

This practice was carried on for many years, in fact until the troubles in the reign of King Charles I. We find letters dated from the Savoy by the Earl of Huntingdon, the Earl of

Cumberland, the Earl of Northampton, the Earl of Rutland, and the other executors of the Duke of Buckingham ; but more especially by George Lord Carew, who seems to have continued to live here while he was Master General of the Ordnance and after he was elevated to the earldom of Totness in 1626. His last letter from the Savoy was written in the year of his death, 1629.

The Earl of Northampton is the Lord Compton mentioned in Dr. Montaigne's list. He was elevated to the higher title in 1618, and appears to have continued his residence here until his death in 1630. Two of his infant children, Elizabeth and Lady Mary, were buried in the Chapel, the first in 1629, before her father became an Earl, the second in 1634. The romantic story of his marriage with the heiress of Lord Mayor Spencer is well known, and need not be repeated here.

Sir George Manners, who lodged by the Water Gate, was brother of the Earl of Rutland, who may therefore have dated from his brother's lodgings. The Duke of Buckingham, whose house, hard by, has been noticed above, was George Villiers, the favourite of James I., and married the daughter and sole heiress of this Lord Rutland. Sir George Manners succeeded his brother as Earl in 1632. The Mr. Roger

Manners, also named above, was of the same family, no doubt, but cannot have been another brother. The Earl of Exeter, already noticed, married Lady Elizabeth Manners, the first cousin of Sir George and the Earl.

Among Lord Carew's letters is one which explains the state of things on the promotion of Dr. Montaigne to the bishopric of Lincoln in 1617. By the removal of the Dean of Westminster, he says, the mastership of the Savoy is likewise void. They say it is to be bestowed upon the Archbishop of Spalato, though one " Belkanque, a Scottish man, pretends a promise in it. I doubt the place be of no great worth, yet somewhat hath some favour. I hear the Archbishop is to preach to-morrow at Mercer's chapel. I will do what I can not to fail to be there."

The rivals here introduced require a few words each, for both became Masters, and one is among the most extraordinary figures of that period. We may take the "Scottish man" first, as there is not much to be said about him. In 1615 his name makes its appearance on the page of history. There is a warrant under the King's own hand in that year for the payment of £200 to Walter Balcanquall. No reason is assigned, and it is useless to conjecture what secret service may have been performed for the

money.   In December 1617 Balcanquall is
made Master of the Savoy.   In 1618 (Jan. 3)
he is made Clerk of the Closet, and the Savoy
is given to the Archbishop.   During the same
month Balcanquall is back at the Savoy, confirmed in the Mastership for life.   On the 25th
March, not two months later, he resigns it.
Just four years afterwards he is again appointed,
having meanwhile continued to be a brother of
the house.   In 1624 he married Lady Ham-
mond, a widow.   In 1625 (March 5) he is
promoted to the Deanery of Rochester.   He
attended the celebrated Synod of Dort, and
seems to have had decided views on theolo-
gical questions.   But his promotion was, no
doubt, owing to his fidelity to Buckingham, of
which he makes boast in a letter to Conway, in
1627, and to his persistence in asking.   He
was always asking ; and by dint of flying at high
game, succeeded in pitching upon the lower at
last.

A very curious letter of his is dated in January
1627.   If the King, he says, will make him
Bishop of Carlisle he will resign the Deanery
of Rochester and the vicarage of Goudhurst,
together worth £360 per annum ; but if the
King will let him keep " his parsonage and
vicarage " he will part with the mastership of
the Savoy and the Deanery of Rochester.   For

the Bishopric of St. David's or Exeter, he would part with the Deanery and Goudhurst. Thus, this pluralist Puritan was Dean of Rochester, Master of the Savoy, Vicar of Goudhurst, " parson " of some parish not named, but probably Adisham, and chaplain to the King. In 1629 he excuses himself for not keeping his month of attendance at Court because he has broken his leg.

At length, after years of waiting, he obtained, not a bishopric indeed, but a better deanery than Rochester, being promoted to Durham, in 1639. It is probable, whatever may have been the nature of his claims on James I., that Charles I. did not acknowledge them. Buckingham's assassination in 1629 removed another patron ; and he must have been thankful for even the Deanery of Durham.

The Archbishop of Spalato, who, as we have seen held the office of Master for a time, has been the subject of much notice, yet I cannot find that any very complete account of him has ever been written. Here, it will not be possible to do much more than detail his connection with the Savoy.

CHAPTER X.

⚇ꝑe 𝔄rcꝑbⅰsꝑop of 𝔖palato.

The Archbishop of Spalato—His coming to England—
His reception—Solomon and the Queen of Sheba—
The Archbishop's Sermon at Mercer's Chapel—His
corpulence—Appointed to the Savoy—His resignation and departure—His tragical end—Conflicting
accounts of his character—Balcanquall restored—
Papists at the Savoy—Balcanquall's promotion and
death.

MARK ANTHONY DE DOMINIS was born at Arba
in Dalmatia in 1566. He was educated at
Loretto by the Jesuits, and proceeded to the
university of Padua, where he very soon distinguished himself, both as a student and as a
lecturer. He studied mathematics and physics
in particular, to such purpose that he was the
first philosopher to give a satisfactory explanation of the phenomenon of the rainbow.

While still a young man he was made a
bishop on the recommendation of the Emperor

Rodolph. His first see was Segni, but within two years he was promoted to the Archbishopric of Spalato, the capital city of his native province. It is under the name of "Spalato" that he is usually spoken of by his contemporaries, as if that was his surname. A contest between Pope Paul V. and the Venetian government as to ecclesiastical endowments seems first to have brought him forward in political life. He warmly espoused the Venetian side, wishing, as he professed, to reform the priesthood, and, indeed, elaborating very carefully a scheme which would have wholly altered most of the controversial questions of the seventeenth century. Since his time similar schemes have been put forward from within the Church of Rome, but with no more success than attended his.

The Archbishop of Spalato.

In 1615, despairing of success, or frightened by the threats and the unscrupulous character of his adversaries, he determined to accept an invitation to England. He resigned his archbishopric and set out, reaching Dover in December 1616. He seems to have been specially patronised by Carleton, the Secretary, and was immediately received with honour by the English Church. He was lodged in Lambeth Palace, and the bishops made up a kind of guarantee fund to give him £600 a year until he obtained preferment. Though we read that

Spalato's coming to England.

The Arch-bishop of Spalato.

his luggage was thrown overboard in a storm between Margate and the Thames, he seems to have been very well provided, and to have kept a retinue of servants befitting his rank.

Spalato's reception.

Immediately on his arrival he professed himself opposed to the claims of papal supremacy, and openly conformed to the Church of England. Archbishop Abbot recommended him to live at one of the universities in a moderate way; but Spalato seems to have preferred London, and we hear on the 31st December, soon after his arrival, that he has been received by the King, and is greatly pleased with the favours bestowed upon him. In a letter to Carleton he compares

Solomon and the Queen of Sheba.

himself to the Queen of Sheba, and "finds the greatness of Solomon more than even it was reported."

In the same letter he mentions his forthcoming work on an *Ecclesiastical Republic*, and it was published in the following year with a dedication to King James, and a fine portrait of the author by Elstracke, which, indeed, is now sought for as a thing of considerably greater value than the book it adorns.

The Arch-bishop's sermon at Mercer's Chapel.

Meanwhile, he preached a sermon in Italian at the Mercer's Chapel in November 1617. It was afterwards printed in English. "A great concourse of Lords and others" was there, says Sir Gerard Herbert in a letter to Carleton.

The sermon, action, manner, and all he said, were very well liked. "When next he preacheth," adds Herbert, "his audience assuredly will be very great. So earnest was he in his labour, as, through his being all in a holy sweat, he was fain to shift linen ere entering the coach to go to dine with my Lord of Canterbury. My Lord of Canterbury saw him enter the coach, and helped him in himself ere entering himself." Archbishop Abbot alludes to the unwieldy bulk of the Dalmatian prelate in another letter. In December he assisted in consecrating at Lambeth Felton, Bishop of Bristol, and Montaigne, Bishop of Lincoln.

At Oxford and Cambridge the Archbishop was received with enthusiasm. Honorary degrees were conferred upon him, and he expressed himself highly gratified with "courtesies whose very number prevented his receiving them properly." As to preferment there was some delay. He was nominated to the Savoy, but Balcanquall had already secured his own induction, and in January 1618 he complained that, like Esau, he was supplanted by Jacob. He has many good words, he says, but as to promotion, he is like the sick man in the porch who had no one to throw him into the waters. A few days after this, however, no doubt through Carleton's good offices, Bal-

The Archbishop of Spalato.

Spalato's corpulence.

Spalato appointed to the Savoy.

canquall took the clerkship of the closet, and resigned the Savoy in favour of the Archbishop. Of his connection with the Savoy we have little notice. He probably never came into residence there, and except for some dispute about a lease, we do not know that he actively interfered in the government of the charity. A month later than the date of Balcanquall's resignation he was still in doubt as to his appointment, but seems to have been meanwhile assiduous in courting the royal favour, and the King is reported in March as being "very desirous of pleasing him." The Deanery of Windsor having fallen vacant, he was promoted to it, and is also said to have received a prebend at Canterbury, but I do not find the fact recorded in Le Neve.

We hear of several sermons at the Mercer's Chapel, where an Italian Protestant congregation was then assembled, but their success was not commensurate with the first. His greed for preferment and other causes seem, before the end of 1618, to have already undermined

his popularity. In March 1623 he resigned the Mastership, and Balcanquall, as we have seen, was re-appointed.

De Dominis now practically disappears from our history, but it may be worth while to summarise the remaining events of his life and his tragical death. His resignation of the Savoy was caused by a determination to return to Rome, where an old friend and schoolfellow of his had just been elected Pope under the name of Gregory XV. He left England immediately, expecting to be made a cardinal, but in this he was disappointed, and on the death of the Pope shortly after, he was seized and imprisoned in the Castle of St. Angelo. It was said that before leaving England he recanted his opinions a second time, and a book published in the Low Countries led to the English looking upon him as an apostate. The authenticity of this book has always been disputed, and the truth cannot now be easily ascertained. Bishop Cosin says he never recanted, and reports that on his departure he openly promised " to confess his faith before the Pope," adding that this promise he faithfully kept. Cosin's opinion would appear to be correct. Certain it is that he was persecuted and imprisoned, and the story that he was "barbarously used" is so far justified by his death, which took place in 1624, in the dungeon in which he was confined. His dead body was solemnly condemned in the presence of his relatives, and was burnt by the common executioner, together with his books.

The whole story of his life has yet to be written, as a curious episode in the history of

The Archbishop of Spalato.

Spalato's tragical end.

Conflicting accounts.

what is called the Romish Controversy. It has even been asserted by an eminent Papist writer, the late Mr. Husenbeth, that before he left England he preached a sermon condemning the reformed opinions he had here professed; and that this sermon led to an order from King James to leave the kingdom in three days. There is no proof adduced in support of this story, and in the face of the records from which our information is derived, it must be untrue.* ·

In 1623, when the proposals for the Spanish marriage of Prince Charles were still being negotiated, a scheme was put forward for assigning the chapel of the Savoy to the use of the retinue of the Infanta, but with the marriage itself, it

soon fell to the ground. In 1626 Conway, the Secretary of State, wrote to Balcanquall calling his attention to information given that there was a place within the Savoy "where masse is usually sayd and much· resort of people to it." The Master is desired to find out the truth of the report, to cause the priest or other ecclesiastical persons to be apprehended, and to seize upon "all the Popish bookes and Massinge stuffe that shall be found there."

* *Notes and Queries*, II. S., viij., 33 and *passim*. There is a biography by the late Dean Newland, but it adds nothing to our knowledge, and is little more than a controversial essay.

Balcanquall was already Dean of Rochester, having been appointed in the beginning of 1625. In 1639 he became Dean of Durham, and dying on Christmas day, 1645, was buried at Chirk in Denbighshire.

During the Commonwealth a meeting of the Independents was held at the Savoy—in October 1658—when a uniform confession of faith was drawn up for publication. During this period also, a congregation of French Protestants obtained leave to assemble in the precinct, and eventually, as we shall see, became established there, though not without opposition.

CHAPTER XI.

The End of the Hospital.

Gilbert Sheldon, Master—The Savoy Conference—The
French Chapel—Tune " Savoy "—The Condition of
the Hospital — Henry Killegrew, Master — The
Jesuit School—The King's Printers—The Sanctu-
ary—An unfortunate Tailor—Condition of the
Hospital at Killegrew's death—Lord Keeper Wright
dissolves it—The Savoy in 1739—Jacob Tonson—
The German Church and the Washerwoman—
Prisoners—Waterloo Bridge—The last ruins disap-
pear.

AFTER the death of Balcanquall in the midst of
the civil commotion which marked the con-
clusion of the reign of Charles I., the Savoy
seems to have had no Master until the Restoration. The house became a refuge for foreigners
and Roman Catholics, and we have complaints
of violence used by the officers of justice in the
pursuit of offenders, especially offenders against
the ecclesiastical laws.

Immediately on the restoration of Charles II. a petition was presented by one Thomas Warmstry, Doctor of Divinity, praying that in consideration of the manifold losses that the petitioner had undergone, owing to his faithful allegiance to the royal cause, he should be appointed Master of the Savoy. Dr. Warmstry, though he appears from another and later petition to have secured the favour of General Monk, did not succeed, owing to the superior claims of a far more famous man. Gilbert Sheldon seems to have obtained a promise of the office during the King's exile. He was at that time a prebendary of Gloucester, and had been Warden of All Souls at Oxford before the Commonwealth.

Immediately on the King's return he. was restored to the Wardenship, and made Dean of the Chapel Royal. To these offices that of Master of the Savoy was added, and before the end of the year he became Bishop of London, being consecrated in Henry the Seventh's Chapel on the 28th of October. He retained the Savoy for the time at least, and in 1661 the celebrated Savoy Conference was held in his lodgings here.

This was a meeting between the restored Churchmen and the Presbyterian party, and was called together by a royal commission, which

The end of the Hospital.

Gilbert Sheldon, Master.

The Savoy Conference.

L

summoned twenty-one divines on each side,
among whom were Archbishop Frewen of York,
Bishops Cosin, Henchman, Morley, Sanderson,
Walton, Gauden, with Heylin, Pearson, and
Sparrow on the side of the Church. Among the
Presbyterian divines summoned were Reynolds,
who had just been made Bishop of Norwich;
Calamy, to whom the Bishopric of Lichfield had
been offered; Baxter, who had been offered
Hereford; Manton, nominated for the Deanery
of Rochester; together with Clarke, Newcomen,
Rawlinson, and Lightfoot.

The commissioners were empowered to con-
fer upon the Book of Common Prayer, its
several directions, rules, and forms; to advise
and consult upon the several objections and
exceptions raised against the same; and to
make such reasonable and necessary alterations
and corrections as should be agreed upon, for
the satisfaction of tender consciences and the
restoring and continuance of peace and unity in
the Church.

" The commission," to quote the summary of
Mr. Blunt,* " met at the Savoy in the Strand
on April 15, and its sittings ended on July 24
1661; the Session of Parliament and Convoca-

---

* *Annotated Book of Common Prayer,* in which a
very complete account of the whole conference may be
found.

tion commencing on May 8 of the same year. The 'several objections and exceptions' raised against the Prayer Book were presented to the Bishops in writing. These are all on record in two or three contemporary reports of the Conference, and they are printed at length in Cardwell's *Conferences on the Book of Common Prayer.* Many of the exceptions are of a frivolous kind, and the remarks which accompanied them were singularly bitter and uncharitable, as well as diffuse and unbusiness-like. It seems almost incredible that grave Divines should make a great point of 'The Epistle is written in' being an untrue statement of the case when a portion of a prophecy was read and *technically* called an 'Epistle;' or that they should still look upon it as a serious grievance when the alteration conceded went no farther than 'For the Epistle;' or, again, that they should spend their time in writing a long complaint about the possibility of their taking cold by saying the Burial Service at the grave. Yet sheets after sheets of thin paper were filled with objections of this kind, and with long, bitter criticisms of the principles of the Prayer Book. The bishops replied to them in the tone in which Sanderson's Preface to the Prayer Book is written, but they seem to have keenly felt what Sanderson himself expressed—mild and gentle as he was—when he long afterwards said of his chief opponent at the Savoy, 'that he had never met with a man of more pertinacious confidence and less abilities, in all his conversation.' Perhaps, too, they were reminded of Lord Bacon's saying respecting his friends, the Nonconformists of an earlier day, that they lacked two principal things, the one learning and the other love.

"The Conference was limited by the letters patent to four months' duration, but when that time had drawn to an end little had been done towards a reconciliation of the objectors to the use of the Prayer Book. Baxter had composed a substitute for it, but even his friends would not accept it as such, and probably Baxter's Prayer Book never won its way into any congregation of Dissenters in his lifetime or afterwards. In Queen Elizabeth's time Lord Burleigh had challenged the Dissenters to bring him a Prayer Book made to fit in with their own principles; but when this had been done by one party of Dissenters, another party of them offered six hundred objections to it, which were more than they offered to the old Prayer Book. The same spirit appears to have been shown at the Savoy Conference ; and the principle of unity was so entirely confined to unity in opposition, that it was impossible for any solid reconciliation of the Dissenters to the Church to have been made by any concessions that could have been offered."

The end of the Hospital.

Eventually, a list was drawn up by the Churchmen of those changes to which they were willing to submit. They are chiefly rather verbal than doctrinal, and are given by Mr. Blunt at length ; many or most of them being afterwards recommended to convocation and adopted.

The last event of importance in the history of the Hospital was the sitting of the Conference.

The French Chapel.

The next few years are only marked by a petition against the establishment of the French congregation within the precinct. One, "Mr. d'Espagne," we read, "upon pretence at first to preach in the house of the Lady Annandale, did after erect a new church without any authority or licence" from Charles I., and a rival congregation in the city was much disturbed by what they looked on as an invasion of their rights. The new congregation assembled at first in the chapel of Somerset House, to which they were admitted by Cromwell. On the Restoration their pastors, whose names are given as Kerhuel and Hierome, sought for leave to open another chapel in the Savoy. The petition was referred to the Archbishop of Canterbury, who, probably concluding that there was room for both

The end of the Hospital. chapels, seems to have permitted the completion of this one, which received a formal patent from the King on 11th March 1661. It has ever since subsisted, not indeed in the Savoy, as, when the approaches to Waterloo Bridge were made, it was removed, and is now, though still under the old name, in Bloomsbury.

Tune "Savoy." It has sometimes been conjectured, and not without reason, that it is to this church that we owe the introduction to popular notice of the well-known old French tune for the 100th Psalm, which often goes by the name of the Savoy. In Mr. Havergal's learned book on the subject* he conjectures that the name refers to its supposed Savoyard origin ; and I do not know that the above theory has ever before been put forward in print. It is, however, so plausible, and tallies so well with the facts of its history, that we may well allow it to be correct, until at least we meet with a better. True, the tune appears in Psalters long before the date of the building of the French Chapel of the Savoy, but this name is not applied to it until about the period of which we are speaking, when the singing in the Chapel caused it to be filled with a large congregation, English as well as French.

We have also, in 1660, a petition from Captain

* *A History of the Old Hundredth Psalm Tune,* by the Rev. W. H. Havergal.

Richard Braywood, an old royalist soldier, asking for the porter's place and "the Barre in the Savoy which they sell drinke at to the lame souldiers." In the following year we hear of William Rumbold, who obtained from the Secretary of State a warrant to search for goods stored in the Savoy, and said to have belonged to the late King, to Cromwell, and other personages. After this, there is a petition from John Price of East Barnet complaining that the room at Mr. Trapham's, which he had hired for the storage of some household stuff, had been broken into by a Major Peter Williams, who threatened to take the goods away, on the ground that they belonged to persons excepted from the Act of Oblivion.

From these and other such-like passages we can see that the condition of the Hospital was gradually deteriorating. A finishing stroke seems to have been put by a great fire which took place in 1661, when the houses of the chaplains were burnt, after which time the chaplains never resided within the precincts. A few years later, as we shall see, they all held preferments elsewhere. In 1670 an Act was passed permitting them to grant leases for forty years, and houses were built and occupied on the site.

An almost greater blow than this fire was

received by the appointment, in 1663, of Henry Killegrew as master in succession to Sheldon. By his improvidence, greed, and other bad qualities, the final ruin of the Hospital was effected.

He is usually styled "Doctor Killegrew" in contemporary notices, but I have not been able to find out where he obtained a degree of D.D. He was a younger brother of the notorious Thomas Killegrew, groom of the bed-chamber to Charles II., and elder brother of Lady Shannon, one of that monarch's many mistresses. He had plenty of Court interest in his favour, but does not seem to have ever received any preferment in the Church, but this and a stall at Westminster, to which he was appointed immediately on the Restoration, and which he held, with the mastership, till his death. He was one of the sons of Sir Robert Killegrew by Mary Woodhouse, his wife, a niece of Lord Bacon. In early life, like his brothers, he affected dramatic authorship, but without, as it would seem, much success; but his *Conspiracy: a Tragedy*, which was written for the wedding festivities of Lord Herbert, and published in 1638, without the author's consent, from a false and imperfect transcript, is somewhat sought after by book-fanciers. In 1653 he printed an amended copy under the title of

Palantus and Eudora. He also published
several sermons and volumes of sermons, but
none of them are of much value. On the title-
page of one now before me he is called " Henry
Killegrew, D.D., Master of the Savoy, and
Almoner to his Royal Highnesse." It is dated
1669.

We shall have occasion to mention Dr. Killegrew again in our account of the chapel. He
appears to have resided in the Savoy, and after
his death a Mrs. Killegrew, his second wife
perhaps, continued in the lodgings for several
years.

The period of his incumbency is marked by
a few events worth notice. In 1686 James the
Second built a spacious house in the Savoy,
including a church and a school for the Jesuits.
Lord Macaulay says of it : " The skill and care
with which those fathers had, during several
generations, conducted the education of youth
had drawn forth reluctant praises from the
wisest Protestants. Bacon had pronounced the
mode of instruction followed in the Jesuit
colleges to be the best yet known in the world,
and had warmly expressed his regret that so
admirable a system of intellectual and moral
discipline should be employed on the side of
error. It was not improbable that the new
academy in the Savoy might, under royal patron-

age, prove a formidable rival to the great foundations of Eton, Westminster, and Winchester. Indeed, soon after the school was opened, the classes consisted of four hundred boys, about one half of whom were Protestants. The Protestant pupils were not required to attend mass, but there could be no doubt that the influence of able preceptors, devoted to the Roman Catholic Church, and versed in all the arts which win the confidence and affection of youth, would make many converts.

"These things produced great excitement among the populace, which is always more moved by what impresses the senses than by what is addressed to the reason. Thousands of rude and ignorant men, to whom the dispensing power and the Ecclesiastical Commission were words without a meaning, saw with dismay and indignation a Jesuit college rising on the banks of the Thames, friars in hoods and gowns walking in the Strand, and crowds of devotees pressing in at the doors of temples where homage was paid to graven images."

This school was dissolved immediately on the abdication of King James II. The scurrilous ballads of the day allude to the sale of the furniture, and make fun of the "massing stuff" and relics. The clock, according to Strype, was said to have been afterwards set up at a gentleman's house at Low Leyton, in Essex.

In 1675 the dormitory was used for sick and wounded soldiers and sailors; and a little later their place was supplied by a regiment of soldiers, whose barrack was one of the last of the domestic buildings destroyed. It stood close to the southern end of the chapel.

In 1669, or before it, the King's printers set up their presses here, and we find "In the Savoy" as the colophon of a large number of Bibles printed before the end of the century. Besides these, many proclamations were printed here, including that by the peers of the realm in 1688, requiring all persons to keep the peace during the interregnum which followed the flight of King James.

Soon after the accession of William and Mary the condition of the Savoy attracted notice. Under Dr. Killegrew it had become a refuge for all kinds of bad characters. When, in 1697, a bill was passed abolishing its privileges of sanctuary, such as they were, there followed "a tumultuous flight to Ireland, to France, to the colonies, to vaults and garrets in less notorious parts of the capital." To quote again from Macaulay, who also draws a striking picture of the condition to which the precinct had now fallen :—

The end of the Hospital.

The King's Printers.

The Sanctuary.

*The end
of the
Hospital.*

An unfor-
tunate
Tailor.

"The Savoy was another place of the same
kind " as Whitefriars, "smaller indeed, and less
renowned, but inhabited by a not less lawless
population. An unfortunate tailor, who ventured
to go thither for the purpose of demanding
payment of a debt, was set upon by the whole
mob of cheats, ruffians, and courtesans. He
offered to give a full discharge to his debtor,
and a treat to the rabble, but in vain. He had
violated their franchises, and this crime was
not to be pardoned. He was knocked down,
stripped, tarred and feathered. A rope was
tied round his waist. He was dragged naked
up and down the street amidst yells of 'A
bailiff! a bailiff!' Finally, he was compelled
to kneel down and to curse his father and
mother. Having performed this ceremony, he
was permitted—and the permission was blamed
by many of the Savoyards—to limp home without a rag upon him. The Bog of Allen, the
passes of the Grampians, were not more unsafe
than this small knot of lanes, surrounded by
the mansions of the greatest nobles of a flourish-
ing and enlightened kingdom."

Condition
of the
Hospital at
Killegrew's
death.

At the date of Killegrew's death in March
1699, the senior chaplain, John Hook, a non-
juror, appointed as long before as 1663, was
living at Basingstoke, where he ministered to a
dissenting congregation; John Lamb, the next

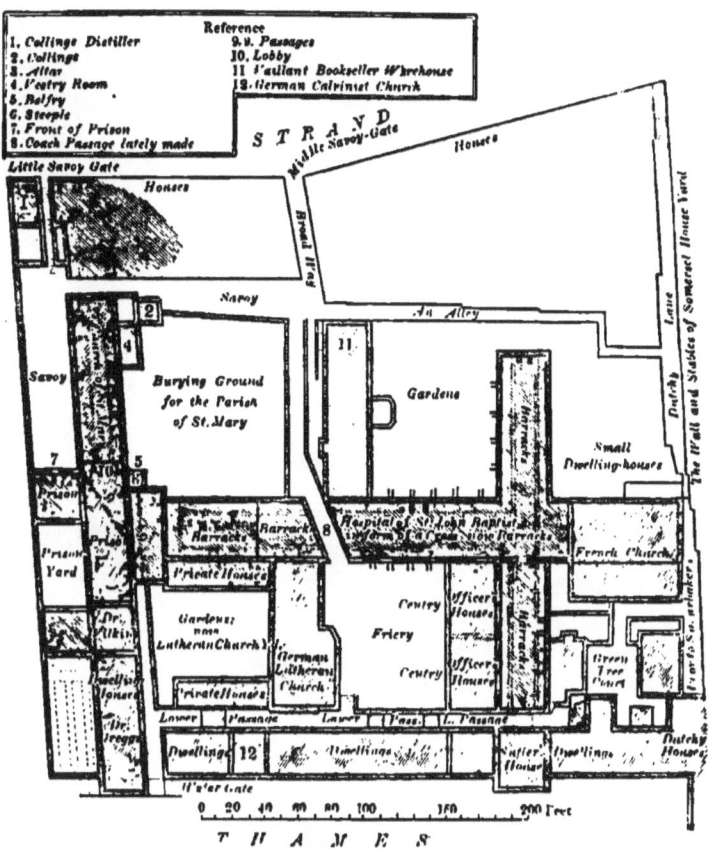

Reference
1. Collings Distiller
2. Collings
3. Altar
4. Vestry Room
5. Belfry
6. Steeple
7. Front of Prison
8. Coach Passage lately made
9. &c. Passages
10. Lobby
11. Vaillant Bookseller Warehouse
12. German Calvinist Church

STRAND

Middle Savoy-Gate

Little Savoy Gate

Houses

Houses

Broad Wall

Savoy

An Alley

Lane

The Wall and Stables of Somerset House Yard

Burying Ground
for the Parish
of St. Mary

Gardens

Duchy

Barracks

Small
Dwelling-houses

Savoy

Prison

Prison
Yard

Dr.
Atkins

Dwelling
House

Dr.
Reggs

Barracks

Private Houses

Gardens;
now
Lutheran Church

Private Houses

Lower

Dwellings

Barracks

Hospital of St. John Baptist
German St. John Baptist Barracks

Gentry

Friery

German
Lutheran
Church

Gentry

Passage

12

Dwellings

Officer
Houses

Officer
Houses

Passes

French Church

Green
Tree
Court

Ferry to St. Saviours

L. Passage

Dwellings

Sutler
House

Dwellings

Duchy
Houses

Water Gate

0 20 40 60 80 100   150   200 Feet

T H A M E S

PLAN OF THE SAVOY PRECINCT IN 1736.

in order, was Dean of Ely, and held various other preferments; Nicholas Onely, the third, was a prebendary of Westminster Abbey and curate of St. Margaret's, as well as rector of Cottesmore in Rutlandshire; and the fourth, Lionel Coles, who was now about thirty-nine years of age, was rector of Bassingborne in Cambridge-shire. It will have been seen that none of the four resided at the Savoy; in fact, their burnt lodgings had never been rebuilt, and a little later we find them occupied by poor houses. Dining in the Common Hall had never been revived after the Restoration. There were four sisters who drew their annual pensions as well as a surgeon, a solicitor, a plumber, and a porter. The revenues had, on the whole, increased since Thurland's time, and now amounted to £386 : 13 : 7. All the hospital had been leased out in tenements except the great cross building (shown in the plan), which was occupied by soldiers and a military hospital, and called the barrack. The Master's house and the chapel were alone devoted to their original purposes. The Master appropriated the profits of these leases and the fines on renewals, and kept no accounts. No visitation of the distant estates was habitually made.

Almost all the furniture and plate had disappeared. In the Master's house there was some tapestry and three old pictures, one of which, a small Holy Family of the early Siennese school, was recently discovered at Hereford, and purchased by Mr. White.

This account of the condition of the Hospital was rendered by the chaplains to Lord Keeper Wright in 1702. A couple of years previously the Savoy had been visited by the Archbishop of Canterbury, with the Bishops of London, Worcester, and Salisbury, and other commissioners, who drew a scheme of reform, to which, as it was never adopted, we need not advert at very great length, but its chief features seem to have been to place the minister of the chapel on the foundation as a brother, and to annex the Mastership to the bishopric of Gloucester.

These visitations and various other proceedings occupied a long time, and the end was further delayed by the death of King William III. on the 8th March 1702. There must have been much trouble in preparing schedules of the estates, as well as lists of the vast miscellaneous population which had gathered in the old precinct. Dr. Killegrew, in his long incumbency, had granted not fewer than thirty leases of tenements and houses built on the site of the Hospital and its offices, most of them for forty years, but some for sixty. These leases, which were many of them of almost nominal rents, had still several years to run, and no attempt seems to have been made to cancel or purchase them.

At length, on the 31st of July 1702, Lord Keeper Wright pronounced the final sentence of dissolution. John Hook and his fellows were deprived as non-resident, and then, since neither Master nor brethren any longer existed, the Hospital itself was declared to be dissolved. This high-handed proceeding was no doubt richly deserved, but it was carried out without a special Act of Parliament, while the recommendation of the Archbishop that a portion of the funds should be applied to the payment of the minister was disregarded, with consequences which will more plainly appear when I come to speak of the chapel. The rents were confiscated to the Crown : a bill to confirm the confiscation passed the House of Commons, but was rejected by the Lords. So late as the time of Lord Chancellor Cowper, an application was said to have been made for the Mastership.

In 1715 the rents had been improved by good management, and raised from the £386, mentioned above, to more than £2000 a year. In 1739 some inquiries were made as to the condition of the precinct, when it was found that a. few of Killigrew's leases still subsisted, and that some of the tenants refused to pay any rent. A parcel of old papers which belonged to the late Peter Cunningham recently came into my hands, in which I find an account of the sitting of the commissioners of 1739. From these papers it appears that several tenants had bought keys, and thereby obtained possession of houses, and neither knew nor cared about the legality of their holding. Among these fortunate people were Jacob Tonson, the famous publisher,

Jacob Tonson.

who had no lease, and paid no rent; and Alexander Cruden (who seems to have been the author of the Concordance), who had once paid a rent of £7 a year, but latterly had paid nothing, and had no lease.

About the same time we find a German, and, strange to say, a Persian, chapel in the precinct. The Persian Ambassador rented a house, and had a mosque, or possibly a Greek Church, in it. The German Chapel, sometimes called the Dutch, as the Dutch Church in Austin Friars is sometimes called German, remained in the Savoy till our own day, and a large burial-ground was attached to it. I have not been able to ascertain the exact date of its foundation, but three years before this commission, namely in 1736,

The German Church and the Washerwoman.

a petition was presented to the Treasury by the German congregation complaining that adjoining their chapel was a very disorderly house kept by the wife of a coal-heaver. She was a washerwoman to the barracks, and much annoyed her neighbours with the stench of the "lye" or washing preparation she used. In addition, she kept pigs, and was, moreover, a person of very ill fame. They obtained eventually a lease of her house at the nominal rent of 3d. a year, and built a vestry on the site. Of another lady we hear that she was called the Queen of the Savoy, but no biographical details have come down to us respecting her.

The barracks have been frequently mentioned. The Marshalsea comes into prominence during the Rebellions of 1715 and 1745. In 1716 thirty-three prisoners arrived in one batch from the north, including Sir Mark Kennaway, Sir Herbert Foult (?), Evan Boteler, gentleman, and other persons of consideration, some of whom seem to have died of their wounds in the adjoining military infirmary.

The building of Waterloo Bridge in 1817 led to the destruction of almost all the remaining buildings. The French Chapel was removed to Bloomsbury. The approaches to the new bridge overwhelmed all the precinct as far west as the site of the great gate, and almost to the German Chapel. The west front of the new Somerset House actually stands within the boundary of the precinct. Lancaster Place

The end of the Hospital.

Prisoners.

Waterloo Bridge.

The end of the Hospital. covers the site of the houses once occupied by the King's printer, by Jacob Tonson and Alexander Cruden; and though some parts of the western wall, covering the warehouse of Messrs. Burgess, existed until 1876, the filling in of the Victoria embankment overwhelmed them also.

The last ruins disappear. Finally, the German Chapel was removed to make way for a new approach to the embankment, and of all the old buildings not a vestige now remains except the Chapel to tell of the site of the once magnificent foundation of King Henry VII. *Perierunt etiam ruinæ.*

CHAPTER XII.

The Chapel.

PEOPLE* pass along the crowded and busy
Strand, some of them for years, without any
acquaintance with the quiet little church, surrounded by green grass and trees, which hides
itself behind the rows of dingy houses. When
the mob, in 1381, broke into the manor-house
of John of Gaunt, it is possible that the chapel

* The portion of this chapter which relates to Thomas
Fuller appeared in my *In and Out of London*, and is here
reprinted by the kind permission of the Society for Promoting Christian Knowledge, together with the woodcut
on p. 236.

The Chapel. so far escaped that its walls and surrounding garth retained their sacred character down to the time of King Henry VII.

It is a fact of importance in this connection to remember that, as we have seen, at least one burial took place here, between the ruin and the restoration. There can be little question that John Sampull, who died in 1510, was actually buried within the chapel; his monument had perished even before the disastrous fire of 1864. He was one of the vicars of St. Stephen's Chapel, in the palace at Westminster, and the inscription on the monument here, preserved by Strype, gives us the further information that he celebrated in the lower chapel of St. Mary. It must not be too decidedly asserted that his burial proves the Savoy Chapel to have been already in existence. Still, as there is a doubt, we may take the benefit of it, and persuade ourselves that the chapel in which we now worship stands on the same ground as that in which Wycliffe may have preached before John of Gaunt.

As to the exact date of the consecration of the new or old church at the building of the hospital, we have no information. It probably took place at or before the time of the ratification of the powers of the trustees of the will of Henry VII., already mentioned.* This was

* P. 96.

on the 14th March 1517 (15$\frac{16}{17}$). But on the
4th July 1516, Pope Leo X. wrote to Cardinal
Wolsey asking him to procure payment from the
King of money due for "letters of plenary indulgence," for the Savoy Hospital. The consecration may have taken place at the arrival of
these letters. That there was some ceremony
of the kind no room is left for doubt, because on another monument, which has also
now disappeared, was this quaint epitaph,
which was perhaps intended for a kind of rude
verse :—

"The first sepulted in this place after they it sacrated
was Humphrey Summerset, deacon, which here does
lye, Batchelour in the Arte, whom cruel death oppressed
the fifteen hundred and fifteenth year of God Almighty,
the fifteenth day of April. Which Humphrey doth call
and cry with lamentable escrikes and good devotion, all
devout Christen Men and Women that pass hereby pray
for my dolorous soul, for Christ's bitter Passion."

The dedication here alluded to was to St.
John the Baptist, and within a very few years
the chapel attained a certain position of importance apart from its connection with the hospital.
The altar was sumptuously furnished. There
were priests and choristers. The great men of
the kingdom came hither to worship, and the
magnificence of the building made it worthy of
its fame.

In 1519 we find among the Records some account of the visit of Henry Courtenay, Earl of Devon, to the chapel. It is probably one example of a great many visits of the nobility. On the 11th March is entered, " Item, for my Lordes servantes bote heyr (hire) from Grenewyche to London to the Savoye, the same time my lorde was confessyd there, xijd. Item, payd the same day for a Bote for my lorde which wayted upon hym from Grenewyche to the Savoye, and from there to my Lord Chamberlayn's to dyner, xvjd. Item, payd for my Lordes servantes dyners at London, the same daye my Lorde was confessyd at the Savoye, xxjd. Item, geven unto my lordes confessor at the Savoye, xijd. Item, for my lordes offeryng at the Savoye, iiijd."

Three other epitaphs * of this sixteenth century, besides those of Sampull and Summerset, also claim a passing notice, though they have now disappeared. One commemorated Humphrey Gosling in lines which are often quoted :—

" Here lieth Humphrey Gosling, of London Vintner,
Of the whyt hart of this parish, a neighbour
Of vertuous behaviour, a very good archer,
And of honest mirth a good company keeper ;

* See *Strype*, also *Seymour's Stowe*, vol. ii. 679, where forty inscriptions from tombs in the chapel are given, for the most part at full length.

So well inclined to Poore and Rich,
God send more Goslings to be sich.
He was servant to the Right Honourable the Lord
Hunsden, Lord Chamberlain, and deceased the 22d
July 1586."

Another relates to John Floid, who was probably a member or master of the choir :—

Situs hic est pietatis ac religionis cultor, Johannes
Floid, Artis Musicæ Bacchalaureus, qui dum vixit, Regis
Henrici Octavi in sacello cecinit, et Christi sepulchrum
invisit Jerosolymis. Ob. Anno Dom. 1523, mensis
Aprilis die tertio.

It will be observed that this pilgrim to the
Holy Sepulchre "took his journey hence to
Heaven" the year after bishops Halsey and
Douglas, to whose tomb we are coming. Floid's
brass is described as "very fair."

The third was of considerable interest; it
stood in the body of the chapel :—

"Of your charity pray for the soul of Humphrey Cook,
citizen and carpenter of London, and master carpenter
of all works to our Sovereign Lord King Henry the
Eighth, and master carpenter of the building of this
Hospital, called the Savoy, the which Humphrey deceased
the 13th day of March in the year of our Lord God 1530,
and lieth under this stone."

In 1522 the oldest monument now remaining
had been placed "before the altar of St. John."
It is a small brass plate, and now lies on a

The Chapel. gravestone in the centre of the chancel. It marks the grave of two bishops, and bears this inscription :—

> Hic jacet, Thomas Halsey Leglinensis Episcopus in Basilica Sancti Petri Romæ nationis Anglicorum peniten-ciarius summæ probitatis vir qui hoc solum post se re-liquit, vixit dum vixit bene. Cui lævus conditur Gavan Dowglas natione Scotus Dunkellensis Presul patria sua exul. Anno Xti 1522.

Bishop Douglas.

This interesting monument * commemorates Gavan Douglas, the celebrated Scottish poet and statesman ; the third son of Archibald "Bell the Cat" Earl of Angus. Among the *State Papers* are several references to his journey into England. The safe conduct was granted in January 1522. He had started from Scot-land, December 13, 1521, and appears to have reached London in February. He was pro-bably at Norham Castle with Lord Dacre on his way, and seems to have been received and lodged at the same nobleman's house, in the parish of St. Clement Danes, when he reached London. It had been supposed that he had lodgings in the Savoy, but in his will he speaks of being "apud hospitium domini Dacris, in

* In December 1873 I read a short paper on it at the Archæological Institute, and have here made use of the same notes. *Arch. Journ.* vol. xxxi. p. 78; also xxx. 203.

partibus Angliæ in parochiæ Sancti Clementis prope Londonium." He directs that his body should be buried in the chapel of the Savoy, and his will, which was dated on the 10th September, was proved on the 19th. He died, it is believed, of the plague, and probably at the same time Bishop Halsey also died of the same epidemic, and so the two prelates are laid side by side, and commemorated on the same brass. Their bodies were seen some years ago in a vaulted grave under the chancel.

Hume of Godscroft, in his *History of the House of Angus*, says of Bishop Douglas, that he left behind him "great approbation of his virtues and love of his person, in the hearts of all good men; for beside the nobility of his birth, the dignity and comeliness of his personage, he was learned, temperate, and of singular moderation; and in those so turbulent times, had always carried himself amongst all the factions of the nobility equally, and with a mind to make peace, and not to stir up parties, which qualities were very rare in a clergyman of those days."

He was certainly one of the first of Scottish poets. From him, according to Warton, Milton was not unwilling to borrow. Some of what he wrote, owing to the ancient dialect in which it is written, is obscure to modern readers, but

The Chapel. all who can understand him agree that his powers were of the first order. I prefer, however, to repeat an anecdote which places his character in a still higher light. In those troubled days it was no unusual thing for the princes of the Church to don the armour of the soldier, and to take up arms in any cause they had at heart. But of Bishop Douglas we read that when the Archbishop of Glasgow, in a conference with Douglas respecting the safety of his nephew, the Earl of Angus, betrayed the fact that under his episcopal robes he wore armour, Douglas reproved him plainly, saying, " We are priests ; it is not lawful for us to bear arms." And leaving him, he informed the Earl that his servants should go with him, and aid him in his escape, but that for himself, he said, " I am a Churchman ; I will go to my chamber and pray for you." And so he did ; and in the end his nephew escaped in safety.

Such was Bishop Douglas. Of his companion in the grave we cannot give so satisfactory an account. It is curious to remark the faint praise with which he is mentioned in his epitaph :—" A man of probity, who left this only behind him, that while he lived he lived well "—words singularly chosen, if it were not intended to cast discredit upon their subject. We shall see by the following extracts from

Wolsey's correspondence that they are true in
both particulars, Halsey having apparently been
noted for his impecuniosity and his luxurious
life.   He left no money, but did leave the
reputation of having loved good living.   The
words of his epitaph, if thus interpreted, have
a curious meaning.   Otherwise, they only
resemble Baker's account of Queen Matilda :
" Of whom nothing remarkable is to be recorded except that nothing remarkable is recorded of her."

The little sentence upon Douglas is far more
interesting.   Scotland was a long way from
England in those days.   Douglas, however
great at home, was here but little known.   The
strange story of his life, of his political struggles,
of the closeness of his connection with the
brother-in-law of King Henry,—these things and
others were only known to a few when special
correspondents wrote in cipher to the Lord
Chancellor, and there were no newspapers.
" An exile from his fatherland " is a poetical
epitaph on a poet.

In 1513 the Bishop of Leighlin, in Ireland,
one Nicholas Maguire, died, and Thomas
Halsey was appointed by the Pope to the
vacant see, at the request, not of Cardinal
Wolsey, but at that of Cardinal Bainbridge,
Wolsey's predecessor in the see at York.   Hal-

The Chapel. sey, who probably went to Rome with Bainbridge in 1511, seems to have made no effort to visit his diocese. He certainly was at Rome in 1514, when his patron died, as it was alleged, by poison. Halsey may have shown caution in not going to Ireland, especially as he was not a native, but Rome does not seem to have been much safer. If Archbishop Bainbridge was poisoned at Rome, which is probable, it is certain that Halsey's successor at Leighlin, Maurice Doran, was murdered in 1525, by his own archdeacon, whom he had reproved for some irregularity. Halsey was still at Rome in 1516, when, on the 14th October, we find Thomas Colman writing to Wolsey to announce his own election to the mastership of the Hospital of St. Thomas of Canterbury, otherwise known as the English College, in which, by the way, Cardinal Bainbridge had been buried ; and complaining that Cardinal Hadrian, the papal collector, had in his house two Englishmen ; one styling himself the Bishop of Leighlin, and the other named John Pennant. He goes on to say that they have abused him for demanding a debt of 288 crowns which they owed to the hospital, and concludes with the elegant sentiment that he hopes to recover the money, because " he who spits in the face of heaven spits on his own beard."

It is doubtful whether he ever got the money. The bishop seems to have been very poor then and for some time afterwards. In February 1517 Bishop de Giglis of Worcester, the English Ambassador at Rome, wrote to Ammonius, the Latin secretary of Henry VIII., to announce the death of Colman and to regret that there was no person fit to succeed him, the bishop of Leighlin being an idle voluptuary and Pennant a fool. He makes the same announcement to Wolsey, and asks for his instructions. Wolsey seems to have replied by asking him to recommend some one for the post, and in January of the following year we have him writing about Halsey in a somewhat different strain. He begins by telling the minister he did not wish to be *fastidious* with him, whatever that may mean, and refers to his chaplain Mr. Bassett, to whom he had probably given a private verbal message qualifying the letter. He goes on, however, in the letter to urge Wolsey to give him a speedy answer. The appointment must be made by the 3d May, and he wants such an authority as he can show the brethren of the Hospital. Next he speaks of Halsey as a claimant of the office. Thomas, Bishop of Leighlin, he says, is at Rome, with nothing to live upon except the penitentiaryship mentioned in the epitaph, " of the which a may not live scantly

The Chapel. with a servant or t[wo]," having been deceived by the late cardinal of York—as to the emoluments perhaps,—and Cardinal Hadrian ; he is a good prelate and knows the language of the court perfectly. This faint praise reads strangely after the previous assertion that Halsey was "an idle voluptuary." Then follows a message from Halsey himself, who had probably persuaded the envoy to write in his favour. He says he will be glad to enter into Wolsey's service and to look after "evil-disposed clerks which come yearly from England to be made priests, and so by they made clandestine with false tittyls." I need hardly say Halsey was never made Master, and long afterwards the office was still vacant, the affairs of the College being administered by Ellis Bodley, one of the brethren.

Meanwhile Halsey found a friend in Cardinal Campeggio who, in 1518, brought him to England in his train. On the 23d July, being Friday, the cardinal legate and his suite landed at the Dele beside Sandwich, and proceeded to Canterbury, where they visited the sights described soon after by Erasmus and remained till Monday, when they proceeded to Boxley Abbey and on Tuesday to Otford, where the magnificent manor-house of Archbishop Warham was situated. Here they rested two days, their host having made great preparations for their reception. They reached Lewisham on Thursday, when there was a halt, and the great officials of London and the State came out to meet him. Bishop Halsey is mentioned as among those who accompanied him.

In 1519 Halsey is back at Otford, and takes part in the consecration of a bishop. His linguistic skill may have recommended him to Cardinal Wolsey, who probably found him useful, and employed him in diplomatic errands to the Continent. Under the date of August 23, 1521 Erasmus mentions an approaching visit from Halsey. He writes to Warham from Bruges that he hopes to have all the news from him. Just a year before the mention of this journey, in August 1520, the Earl of Surrey, afterwards 3d Duke of Norfolk, then Deputy in Ireland, informs Wolsey of the death of the Bishop of Cork and recommends Halsey for that see. Where or how Surrey had made his acquaintance does not appear, but his opinion tallies very well with that formed by Sylvester de Giglis, so at least we may judge by the kind of work for which he is wanted. The Lord Deputy begins by saying that the revenues of Cork are worth 200 marks a year, from which we may judge that Leighlin was poor indeed if Cork was to be promotion from it. He then beseeches

The Chapel. Wolsey that no Irishman may be appointed, "that none of this country have it, nor none other than such as will dwell thereupon and such as dare and will speak and ruffle when need shall be." But Halsey did not get Cork any more than the English Hospital. This is the last we hear of him, except the mention by Erasmus, already quoted. He is said to have died "at Westminster" in Cotton's *Fasti*, which may mean the Savoy. In 1523 his bishopric is given to another.

It is impossible not to remark on the strange irony which has connected these two men together in their death—that one of the greatest prelates of his age, a man almost of royal birth, a poet of the first rank, a minister but lately wielding the highest powers, should be thus linked in the grave with an obscure seminary priest of questionable character, to whom he is indebted by the accident of their common fate for even the parenthetical line which marks his last resting-place.

Consecrations. In 1537 the first consecration of a bishop took place in our chapel, when, on the 19th August, Robert Aldrich, Bishop of Carlisle, here received the laying on of hands from John Stokesley, Bonner's predecessor as Bishop of London, Robert Parfew, Bishop of St. Asaph, and John Hilsey, who had succeeded the great John

Fisher as Bishop of Rochester. As but one other ordination of the kind is on record as having been held in this chapel, it may be as well to notice it here. On the 16th January 1698 Thomas Wilson was consecrated in the Savoy to the Bishopric of Sodor and Man : the officiating bishops were John Sharp, Archbishop of York, Nicholas Stratford, Bishop of Chester, and John Moore, Bishop of Norwich. It is to be observed that both these bishops were con-secrated to sees in the northern province. The Bishop of Sodor was nominated by the Earl of Derby, who was then " King in Man."

The next event of importance in the history of our chapel has had a curious influence on its subsequent fate. The Protector Somerset pulled down the Church of St. Mary le Strand in order to place his great new palace on the site. Somer-set House, though it still bears his name, was not completed in his time. The parishioners were left as sheep without a shepherd. On 8th No-vember 1564, Edmund Grindall, Bishop of London, afterwards Archbishop of Canterbury, writes thus to the Master of the Savoy (Thomas Thurland) :—

" This shall be to certify you that whereas the taking order with the parishioners of Strand to unite them to some parish or parishes hath long hanged in suspense; now both for the

The Chapel. reforming of such points as are out of order in that behalf, and also for the ministering of justice to them that complain on the injuries they suffer through the same disorder, I will, God willing, according to mine office, join them to some place or places. In the which order taking, they that be not lotted unto St. Clement's the next parish, and within the precincts whereof the said Strand is situate, they must be united unto St. Martin's in the Fields, except they do otherwise devise and procure that they be by lawful order appointed to the Savoy, which then must be done by the way of composition from me as the ordinary, and from the Right Honorable Sir William Cecil, patron of St. Clement's, of the which parish the Savoy is an Hospital, and by the consent of you the Master of the Savoy, and also by the consent of the parson of St. Clement's. Wherefore, because that now upon my toleration many of them resort to hear divine service in your house the Savoy; this shall be to request you that upon Sunday next, at service and time convenient, the minister declare unto the said parochiance of Strand, that after one month, ye will no more admit them to come to your church. Whereof I also require you, willing them in the mean time to consult amongst themeselves to frame to some good order for the better leveing hereof. Also if they will, they may to the same end commune with you and with the parson of St. Clement's or vicar of St. Martin's, and the more willingly they conform themselves to decent and lawful order, the less need there is to use any compulsory meanes. And so fare ye well. From my house in London, the eighth day of November 1564.

"Yours in Christ,

"Edmund London."

This letter was shortly followed by an arrangement which made the parishioners of St. Mary's free of the chapel, with leave to appoint a minister for themselves, subject to the Master's approbation. To this arrangement we probably owe the preservation of the chapel when all around it was ruined. The people of St. Mary's used it until 1717, when their new church in the Strand was built, and the chapel gradually acquired a name, sometimes still erroneously given it, of "St. Mary le Savoy." The parishioners seem to have had some relics of the old church which they brought with them; and a rent of £4 : 13 : 4 was annually paid by the chapel wardens for the use of the bell. Of course the bell went away with the parish, and so, though we have a tower, nothing hangs in it.

The names of several of the parish ministers

The Chapel.

The Chapel opened to the parishioners of St. Mary, 1564.

The Chapel.
The
Curates.

have been preserved, and two of them at least were men of the highest eminence. The following list is chiefly taken from Mr. Gwynne's paper already mentioned:—1592, William Biggs, curate; 7th Feb. 1592, John Bigg, "cl. licentiat"; 1607, Michael Culford; 1615, John Larkin, "predicator," and Christopher Trevit, "curat"; 1619-1625, Henry Bagley; 1625-27, Edward Thurman; 1627, George Gillingham; 1630-32, Thomas Hastler; 1633-35, John Maccaber; 1636-37, Henry Pight; 1640, Richard Barker, curate; 1647-49, William Bridgwater; 1664, Westwood; 27th July 1671, Anthony Horneck; 7th April 1697, Samuel Pratt, A.M.

Thomas
Fuller.

Between Bridgwater and Westwood should be placed the name of one of the greatest of the many great men who are connected with the history of the chapel.* There is nothing more remarkable than the way in which the long perspective of past time brings certain figures into prominence, while it suffers others to fall out of sight. When we are near a lighthouse, the waves seem to dash over it, and at times even to conceal it. But when we are farther away the waves are no more seen, while the light shines out clearly and brightly. And so, when we read the life of a good man, when we note the events of his career, when we enumerate

* *In and Out of London*, p. 137.

his friends, and, perhaps, examine the doings of his enemies; while we trace his steps as he surmounted difficulties, and avoided dangers, and fought through obstructions, till he reached the goal, we are often confused among the names and places, the people and scenes, the events and complications by which his course was marked. But when, after a time, we begin to forget his immediate surroundings, when he becomes more of an historical character to us, we are able to estimate his greatness by the way in which his deeds or his words are still like shining lights among us; and as the people among whom he lived and worked become hidden in the obscurity of ages, we are able to observe how his figure comes out from those of its associates, and illustrates the same truth now which centuries ago he strove to point to his contemporaries. It is thus, in a remarkable degree, with the character of Fuller. As the quaint epitaph on his monument at Cranford states, he spent his life making others immortal, and thereby attained immortality himself;—a sentence which is true of him in a double sense, for though the reference is there first to his great work, the *Worthies of England*, it also holds good to the work he performed as a clergyman, and especially to that part of his work which was performed in the Savoy, and

The Chapel. among the predecessors of the congregation who still assemble where he for the last time preached the gospel of peace.

Born in 1608, Thomas Fuller was in the prime of life when the great troubles of the Civil War broke upon this country. He lived one year only after the Restoration, and died at the comparatively early age of fifty-three. His career was thus passed among events and trials sufficient to make most men partisans, and to disturb the most even temperaments. But it is Fuller's greatest praise that, living in the midst of strife, he took no part in it; that nothing shook his faith; that no employment caused him to deviate from the strict path of duty; that the end of his labours was to spread abroad the knowledge of truth, to comfort the fatherless and the widow, to show the cheerfulness of an undaunted Christian spirit; and to make all men know the possibility of moderation, when passion and prejudice were the ruling powers. What his faith was may be learnt from the quaint sentence he has put into one of his epigrams. It refers to his own name, and is a fair specimen of the solemn play on words in which he so much delighted. It is headed "A Prayer:"—

" My Soul is stainèd with a dusty colour,—
Let thy Son be the sope, I'll be the Fuller."

And elsewhere, speaking of his infirmities

being known to God, he says most devoutly, "As for other stains and spots upon my soul, I hope that He (be it spoken without the least verbal reflection) who is the Fuller's sope, Mal. iii. 2, will scour them forth with His merit, that I may appear clean, by God's mercy." And when asked to make an epitaph for himself, it is said that he humbly replied, " Let it be, ' Here lies Fuller's earth.' "

Fuller began his ministrations in the Savoy, according to his latest biographer, Mr. Bailey, in the year 1641, and he remained here at first for three years. He was in London, therefore, in the most exciting times; and his preaching was thought so much of that it was said he had two congregations, one within the church, and the other consisting of those who could not get in, but crowded about the windows and doors to get within reach of his voice. It is possibly in reference to the hour-glass in the pulpit here that he says, speaking of another preacher, Dr. Holdsworth, that "whereas the London people honour their pastors for a short hour, his was measured by a large glass :" a sentence which may be well applied to his own preaching. He used his influence, not in adding to the violence of party feeling, which then ran so high, but in endeavouring by all means in his power to make peace among the contending factions;

and among the sermons of his which are still extant, there is one, preached here with this aim in December 1642, just as the terrible war broke out. He chose for his text the words, "Blessed are the peace-makers," and said, "We are used to *end* our sermons with a blessing : Christ *begins* His with the beatitudes ; and of the eight my text is neither the last nor the least." The *best work*, he says, is *peace-making*, and the best wages, that they who make peace are "*blessed.*" Advocating peace, then, he is careful to be moderate even in this, refusing to ask for peace at any price, but peace without any sacrifice of truth. Yet the sword, he says, is the worst way of finding truth, for "it cannot discern between truth, error, and falsehood ; it may have two edges, but it hath never an eye."

In addition to this sermon, he has left us an essay on *Moderation*, which is well worth reading at the present day. He defines moderation in a few admirable sentences : it "is not a halting between two opinions." . . . "Neither is it a lukewarmness in those things wherein God's glory is concerned. But it is a mixture of discretion and charity in one's judgment." "The lukewarm man," he continues, "eyes only his own ends and particular profit ; the moderate man aims at the good of others and the unity of the church."

Toward the middle of 1643 he was forced to fly from the Savoy. He did so with the utmost regret, following King Charles to Oxford. His last sermon preached in this church before his departure is also still extant, and prefixed to it is an epistle "to my dear parish, St. Mary, Savoy," full of touching allusions to his sorrow at leaving them, and his hope that peace might at length return. "The longer," he says, "I see this war, the less I like it, and the more I loathe it. Not so much because it threatens temporal ruin to our kingdom, as because it will bring a spiritual hardness of hearts. And if this war long continues, we may be affected for the departure of charity, as the Ephesians were at the going away of St. Paul, sorrowing most of all that we shall see the face thereof no more."

Fuller followed the King's army to the field, and endeavoured to do what he could to succour the wounded and comfort the dying. Another preacher took possession of his pulpit here, and he himself, like many of the clergy of his time, when the war was over, wandered from one place to another, patronised by moderate men, and loved by all. He says: "For the first five years during our actual civil wars, I had little list or leisure to write, fearing to be made a history, and shifting daily for my safety. All that time I could not live to study,

The Chapel. but did only study to live." Yet during this time he projected and in part composed his works, the *Church History* and the *Worthies of England ;* the latter, however, not being finished till just before his death. In 1645 he came back to the Savoy for a time, but his own flock was dispersed by the troubles, and it was said of him, as of his Divine Master, " He came to his own, and his own received him not." The few who remained were overawed by the factions which divided London, and were in daily fear between the Presbyterians and the Independents. Yet he preferred a London congregation to any other, for, he said, some clergymen wished for a Lincolnshire church, as best built, and others for a Lancashire parish, as the largest, but he liked a London audience, as consisting of the most intelligent people. He did not stay here long, however. He would not give up the Liturgy, and the penalties for using it were fixed that very year at £5 for the first offence, £10 for the second, and a year's imprisonment for the third. He was, therefore, thrown on his own resources, and his means were very small, and wholly insufficient for the support of himself and the education of his son. Brighter days were in store, and he was allowed to remain unmolested as Vicar of Waltham, and afterwards as Rector of Cranford, until the

Restoration, when we find him again at the Savoy.

But, in the meantime, its precincts had been further consecrated to him by a melancholy event. His friend, Lord Montagu of Boughton, being suspected by the party in power and arrested, was imprisoned, or rather kept in some kind of restraint, in the Savoy, although a person of "great reverence," as we are told, "and above fourscore years of age;" and, after about two years' confinement, he died here. In Fuller's *Worthies* he is thus spoken of:—"To have no bands in their death is an outward favour many wicked have, many godly men want; amongst whom this good Lord, who died in restraint at the Savoy, on account of his loyalty to his Sovereign."

Fuller's return to the Savoy was marked by such a welcome as few preachers have ever been accorded. His sermons, in which he had formerly endeavoured to preserve peace, now that the war was over, were directed to the mitigation of the cruelties of the party in power. Their influence is mentioned by many of his contemporaries, and among others by Pepys, the diarist. Witty as all his utterances were, they were always within bounds. As his biographer says, his wit is all but invariably allied to wisdom, "and very few would rise from the

The Chapel. perusal of his pulpit utterances with a feeling that they had been in the company of one who was irreverent or undevout." Craik said of him, in his *History of English Literature*, that "there is probably neither an ill-natured nor a profane witticism in all that Fuller has written." He was strongly of opinion that sermons should be short, and in his account of an ideal "Faithful Minister," he speaks of him as "one who makes not that wearisome which should ever be welcome;" adding, in his quaint way, an anecdote of a certain professor, "who, being to expound the prophet Esay to his auditors, read 21 years on the first chapter, and yet finished it not."

And now we come to the close. Fuller was made, without solicitation, a Royal Chaplain, and prepared a sermon to preach at court. But it was otherwise ordered. Before the day appointed for its delivery, the preacher had left the pulpit for ever. A greater King had summoned him. On the 12th of August 1661, being Sunday, he preached in the Savoy. It was for the last time. He felt unwell, and his friends would have kept him from making the exertion. But a member of the congregation was to be married on the following day, Monday, and Fuller lovingly undertook to wish the wedding couple well in a special sermon, a good custom which still obtains in the Savoy. He said he "had often gone into the pulpit sick, but always come down well, and he hoped he should do as well now by God's strengthening grace." Before he began, he told his congregation he felt ill,' but by a strong exertion he got through, and, as his biographer records, "he very pertinently concluded." A christening was to have followed, and he would have made an effort to officiate; but the fever had now taken its hold. He was carried from the church half fainting, and being taken to his lodgings, he was put to his bed, and he never rose from it again. So Monday and Tuesday passed, and on Wednesday he was much worse. He had been insensible, but as his strength abated his senses returned. Many friends stood round him. He begged them to pray for him, and joined fervently with them, "recommending himself, with all humble thankfulness and submission, to God's welcome Providence." He would not, as the last scene drew near, allow any one to weep. He begged them to restrain themselves, to refrain from tears, and spoke of his departure as a translation to a happy eternity. Though he had before counselled men to make their wills early in life, that so, when they came to die, they might "have nothing to do but to die," he had made no will himself, having pro-

The Chapel. bably little to leave.   And now he refused to be disturbed by any thought ·of worldly affairs. Even the book by which his name has chiefly lived, and which was still unpublished, he did not speak of at all.   His thoughts were all engaged on the world to which he was hastening. No regret for the career which had so lately been re-opened to him—no sorrow for the loss of the bishopric to which he was already designated—nothing but love to those around him, and hope of the heaven before him.   One more night he lived, and on the morning of Thursday, the 18th, passed away in peace ; and so, as his biographer says, " The last view of the faithful minister represents him as assuming, in place of the lawn of the Prelate, the shining raiment, exceeding white as snow, so as no fuller on earth can white it : a whiteness mixed with no shadow ; a light dimmed with no darkness."

Anthony Horneck.   Scarcely second to Fuller was Anthony Horneck, of whom it was said that his parish extended from Whitechapel to Whitehall, so widespread was his popularity.   Seats, it is traditionally reported, were set outside the windows of our little chapel, that those who could not get in might have a chance of hearing his voice.   We can the more readily believe this statement from what we have seen Sunday after Sunday of late years.

Horneck was not an Englishman, having been born at Bacharach on the Rhine in 1641. He* came to England at the Restoration, and probably went straight to Oxford, where he became Master of Arts in 1664. He gave up the rectory of Dolton in Devonshire in 1671, being licensed Curate of the Savoy on the 29th July in that year. The name of a Thomas Horneck occurs among the list of burials in the Savoy, January 18, 1680, probably a son of the Curate, who had been married shortly after his induction. Dr. Horneck became a prebendary of Westminster in 1693, and on his death in 1697 he was buried in the Abbey.

His preaching is described by Evelyn in his *Diary* (18th March 1683) as most pathetic. He also observes that he led a saint-like life, and commends his treatise on *Consideration*, a volume of devotional meditations, the full title of which runs as follows :—"The great law of Consideration, or a Discourse wherein the nature, usefulness, and absolute necessity of Consideration, in order to a truly serious and religious life, are laid open." Bishop Kidder, who published a memoir of him, prefixed to an edition of his works, says of his sermons that "a

* I am indebted to the admirable notes of Colonel Chester on the Westminster Abbey Register for most of these particulars.

The Chapel. great vein of piety and devotion runs through them ; they savour of the primitive simplicity and zeal, and are well fitted to make men better."

The earliest entry in the Register book of our chapel was made the year before Horneck came to it. The town of Northampton had suffered from a terrible fire, and collections were made in the London churches for the relief of sufferers. The Savoy collection, which was taken on the 22d May 1676, only amounts to " fower pounds fower shillings and fower pence." With this entry we may contrast another made just ten years later. On the 19th May 1686, Dr. Horneck preached on behalf of the distressed French Protestants then in the height of the misery caused by the revocation of the Edict of Nantes. The collection amounted to £35 : 15s. and a few months later, in March 1688, a further sum of £27 : 3s. was gathered for the same purpose. Considering the difference in the value of money, this represents the charity of a large and wealthy congregation, and contrasts strongly with the " fower pounds " of ten years before.

Samuel Pratt. After Horneck's death Samuel Pratt, D.D., was nominated to the curacy by the inhabitants of St. Mary's, and was admitted by Dr. Killegrew to the office on the 7th April 1697. He continued to hold it after the separation of the parish

from the precinct on the building of the church
of St. Mary le Strand. He was also vicar of
Tottenham High Cross, and died in 1731,
when he was succeeded at the Savoy by John
Wilkinson.

CHAPTER XIII.

Poets of the Savoy.

Chaucer—Douglas—Wither—Cowley—Dryden—Mrs. Anne Killegrew—Mr. Pendarvis.

In the first part of this book I had occasion to speak of a great poet who was connected with this place. Chaucer's name may fitly commence a chapter devoted to the poets whose memory still lingers about these ancients walls. Chaucer and Gavan Douglas have a successor here in George Wither, a poet whom his own age neglected, but whom modern readers and admirers of true genius have restored to his right place. He was buried in May 1667, in the ground beneath our feet, no memorial marking his grave. How he came to be buried here I cannot tell : many of his days had been spent in confinement, and this may have entitled him to sleep under the shadow of a prison. This is not the place for the instructive story of his strange life. It does not connect him with the Savoy. But his grave is here, and the hymns of praise he sang are in all the churches. Being dead, he yet speaks, or rather, he yet sings. Among the memories which crowd about us in this place, none is worthier than his. Of all the testimony which has here been borne to the truth, none is nobler. When we endeavour to resolve the cloud of witnesses which compasses us about as we worship in the Savoy Chapel, no figure is better defined. A volume of his hymns, recently reprinted, is entitled "Hallelujah, or Britain's Second Remembrancer; bringing to remembrance (in praiseful and penitential hymns, spiritual songs and moral odes) meditations advancing the glory of God, in the practice of piety and virtue." As a recent writer says of him, "he laboured according to his talent, to set aside profane and immodest songs by restoring the muse to its ancient honour, that of composing songs and hymns for the inculcation of virtue and piety." Not that Wither was incapable of the lighter efforts of poetry. One of his songs is still popular :—

> " Shall I, wasting in despair,
> Die because a woman's fair ?
> Or my cheeks make pale with care
> 'Cause another's rosy are ?

Be she fairer than the day
Or the flowery meads of May,
  If she be not so to me
  What care I how fair she be?

" Shall my foolish heart be pined
'Cause I see a woman kind ;
Or a well disposéd nature
Joinéd with a lovely feature?
Be she meeker, kinder than
Turtle dove, or pelican,
  If she be not so to me
  What care I how kind she be?

" Shall a woman's virtue move
Me to perish for her love?
Or her merit's value known
Make me quite forget mine own?
Be she with that goodness blest
Which may gain her name of Best ;
  If she seem not such to me
  What care I how good she be?

" ' 'Cause her fortune seems too high,
Shall I play the fool and die?
Those that bear a noble mind
Where they want of riches find,
Think what with them they would do
Who without them dare to woo ;
  And unless that mind I see,
  What care I though great she be?

" Great or good, or kind or fair,
I will ne'er the more despair ;
If she love me, this believe,
I will die ere she shall grieve ;

> If she slight me when I woo,
> I can scorn and let her go ;
>   For if she be not for me,
>   What care I for whom she be ? "

Some of his other songs might well be revived also.   Charles Lamb said of Wither that before his day no one had ever celebrated the power of poetry *at home.*   " It seems to have been left to Wither," he continues, " to discover that poetry was a present possession as well as a rich reversion, and that the muse had promise of both lives—of this and of that which was to come."   Wither himself, in speaking of poetry, says :—

> " Her true beauty leaves behind
> Apprehensions in the mind
> Of more sweetness than all art
> Or inventions can impart ;
> Thoughts too deep to be expressed,
> And too strong to be suppressed."

Wither's devotional poetry is scarcely so well known as it should be.   The unhappy circumstances of his life, the constant disappointments which form his history, never clouded his faith, and his best hymns are those of joy and aspiration :—

> " Yea, since Thy mercy from on high
> This joy on us bestowed ;
> Let works of mercy sanctify
> The gladness we have showed.

Let us to those that are distressed,
   A word of comfort speak ;
Relieve the needy and oppressed,
   Add strength unto the weak ;
So God will change our outward mirth
   To such internal joy,
That nothing, whilst we live on earth,
   Our comfort shall destroy."

He never forgets the practical side of the Christian's religious character, and in an age when piety was too often degraded into dogmatism, and devotion into sectarian bitterness, it is refreshing to hear such lines as these from his hymn, quaintly entitled, "For the present day or the last day" :—

" So let us walk, so let us work,
Whilst this fair daylight is possessed,
That when Death's evening waxeth dark,
Our flesh in hope may sweetly rest,
   Until that mortal night be done,
   And day immortal is begun.
And when time's veil is rent away,
Whereby Eternity is hid,
When Thou shalt all things open lay,
Which here we thought, or said, or did ;
   Among Time's ruins bury so
Our failings through our tract of time,
That from these dungeons here below
We to celestial thrones may climb ;
   And then to our Eternal King
   For ever Hallelujah sing."

It is perhaps as well that we know so little of

Wither's connection with the Savoy. It was almost certainly of a painful kind : but whether it was as a prisoner in the Marshalsea or a parishioner of St. Mary le Strand, we know that he was released from an imprisonment of three years in the Tower on the 27th July 1663, giving security for his good behaviour, and nearly four years later, namely on the 2d May 1667 he died, and was buried in our church. *Poets of the Savoy.*

The Savoy seems to have had the power of attracting poets ; about this time it was that Cowley applied for the post of Master, and being refused, wrote his " Complaint," but there is no mention of the Savoy in the poem. Cowley.

Before the fire of 1864 there was a memory here of another and more celebrated poet. We have spoken in a previous chapter, at sufficient length, of Dr. Henry Killegrew, the last master of the hospital, who, succeeding to his office at a period when care and economy could alone have restored the waning fortunes of the institution, bestowed upon it neither the one nor the other. There is a redeeming feature in the story of his connection with the Savoy, a gleam of brightness in the saddest chapter of our history. The master's fair daughter, Anne, must have been a paragon of beauty and genius. If we allow as largely as possible for the exaggerations of the poet, still the heroine of Dryden.

Mrs. Anne Killegrew.

Dryden's noble elegy must have been a lady of more than ordinary accomplishments, and in that age of celebrated beauties, a more than ordinary beauty :—

I.

Thou youngest virgin daughter of the skies,
Made in the last promotion of the blest ;
Whose palms, new-plucked from Paradise,
In spreading branches more sublimely rise,
Rich with immortal green, above the rest :
Whether, adopted to some neighbouring star,
Thou rollest above us in thy wandering race ;
　　Or in procession fixed and regular,
　　Movest with the heaven's majestic pace ;
　　Or, called to more superior bliss,
Thou tread'st, with seraphims, the vast abyss :
Whatever happy region is thy place,
Cease thy celestial song a little space ;
Thou wilt have time enough for hymns divine,
Since heaven's eternal year is thine.
Hear then a mortal muse thy praise rehearse,
　　In no ignoble verse.
But such as thy own voice did practise here,
When thy first-fruits of poesy were given ;
To make thyself a welcome inmate there :
　　While yet a young probationer,
　　And candidate of heaven.

II.

　　If by traduction came thy mind,
　　Our wonder is the less to find
A soul so charming, from a stock so good ;
Thy father was transfused into thy blood :

So wert thou born into a tuneful strain,
An early, rich, and inexhausted vein.
  But if thy pre-existing soul
  Was formed at first with myriads more,
It did through all the mighty poets roll,
  Who Greek or Latin laurels wore,
And was that Sappho last, which once it was before.
  If so, then cease thy flight, O heaven-born mind !
Thou hast no dross to purge from thy rich ore :
Nor can thy soul a fairer mansion find,
  Than was the beauteous frame she left behind :
Return to fill or mend the choir of thy celestial kind.

III.

  May we presume to say, that at thy birth
New joy was sprung in heaven as well as here on earth?
  For sure the milder planets did combine
  On thy auspicious horoscope to shine,
  And e'en the most malicious were in trine.
  Thy brother-angels at thy birth
  Strung each his lyre and tuned it high,
  That all the people of the sky
Might know a poetess was born on earth.
  And then, if ever, mortal ears
Had heard the music of the spheres,
And if no clustering swarm of bees
On thy sweet mouth distilled their golden dew,
  'Twas that such vulgar miracles
  Heaven had not leisure to renew :
For all thy blest fraternity of love
Solemnised there thy birth, and kept thy holiday above.

IV.

O gracious God ! how far have we
Profaned thy heavenly gift of poesy !

Made prostitute and profligate the Muse,
Debased to each obscene and impious use,
Whose harmony was first ordained above
For tongues of angels, and for hymns of love.
O wretched we, why were we hurried down
This lubrique and adulterate age
(Nay, added fat pollutions of our own),
To increase the steaming ordures of the stage—
What can we say to excuse our second fall?
Let this thy vestal, heaven, atone for all :
Her Arethusian strain remains unsoiled,
Unmixed with foreign filth, and undefiled ;
Her wit was more than man, her innocence a child.

V.

Art she had none, yet wanted none,
For nature did that want supply ;
So rich in treasures of her own,
She might our boasted stores defy :
Such noble vigour did her verse adorn,
That it seemed borrowed, where 'twas only born.
Her morals too, were in her bosom bred,
    By great examples daily fed,
What in the best of books, her father's life, she read.
And to be read herself she need not fear ;
Each test, and every light, her muse will bear,
Though Epictetus with his lamp were there
E'en love (for love sometimes her muse exprest),
Was but a lambent flame which played about her breast,
Light as the vapours of a morning dream ;
So cold herself, while she such warmth exprest,
'Twas Cupid bathing in Diana's stream.

VI.

Born to the spacious empire of the Nine,
One would have thought she should have been content

To manage well that mighty government ;
But what can young ambitious souls confine ?
To the next realm she stretched her sway,
For Painture near adjoining lay,
A plenteous province and alluring prey.
A Chamber of Dependencies was framed
(As conquerors will never want pretence
    When armed, to justify the offence),
And the whole fief in right of poetry she claimed ;
The country open lay without defence,
For poets frequent inroads there had made,
    And perfectly could represent
The shape, the face, with every lineament,
And all the large domains which the Dumb Sister
    swayed ;
All bowed beneath her government,
Received in triumph wheresoe'er she went.
Her pencil drew whate'er her soul designed,
And oft the happy draught surpassed the image in her
    mind.
The sylvan scenes of herds and flocks,
The fruitful plains and barren rocks,
Of shallow brooks that flowed so clear,
The bottom did the top appear ;
Of deeper, too, and ampler floods,
Which as in mirrors showed the woods ;
Of lofty trees with sacred shades,
And perspectives of pleasant glades,
Where nymphs of brightest form appear
And shaggy satyrs standing near,
Which them at once admire and fear.
The ruins too of some majestic piece,
Boasting the power of ancient Rome or Greece,
Whose statues, friezes, columns, broken lie,
And though defaced, the wonder of the eye ;

What nature, art, bold fiction, e'er durst frame,
Her forming hand gave feature to the name.
So strange a concourse ne'er was seen before,
But when the peopled ark· the whole creation bore.

VII.

The scene then changed ; with bold erected look
Our martial king the sight with reverence strook :
For not content to express his outward part,
Her hand called out the image of his heart :
His warlike mind, his soul devoid of fear,
His high-designing thought were figured there,
As when, by magic, ghosts are made appear.
Our phœnix queen was portrayed, too, so bright,
Beauty alone could beauty take so right :
Her dress, her shape, her matchless grace,
Here are observed as well as heavenly face.
With such a peerless majesty she stands,
As in that day she took the crown from sacred hands ;
Before a train of heroines was seen,
In beauty foremost, as in rank the queen.
    Thus nothing to her genius was denied,
But like a ball of fire, the further thrown,
Still with a greater blaze she shone,
And her bright soul broke out on every side.
What next she had designed heaven only knows :
To such immoderate growth her conquest rose,
That fate alone its progress could oppose.

VIII.

Now all those charms, that blooming grace,
The well-proportioned shape and beauteous face,
Shall never more be seen by mortal eyes ;
In earth the much lamented virgin lies.

Not wit nor piety could fate prevent ;
Nor was the cruel destiny content
To finish all the murder at a blow,
To sweep at once her life and beauty too ;
But, like a hardened felon, took a pride
To work more mischievously slow,
And plundered first, and then destroyed.
A double sacrilege on things divine,
To rob the relic and deface the shrine !
  But thus Orinda died :
Heaven by the same disease did both translate :
As equal were their souls so equal was their fate.

IX.

Meantime her warlike brother on the seas
His waving streamers to the winds display,
And vows for his return, with vain devotion, pays.
Ah, generous youth ! that wish forbear,
The winds too soon will waft thee here !
Slack all thy sails, and fear to come ;
Alas ! thou know'st not thou art wrecked at home !
No more shalt thou behold thy sister's face,
Thou hast already had her last embrace.
But look aloft, and if thou ken'st from far,
Among the Pleiads a new-kindled star,
If any sparkles than the rest more bright,
'Tis she that shines in that propitious light.

X.

When in mid-air the golden trump shall sound,
To raise the nations under ground ;
When in the valley of Jehoshaphat
The judging God shall close the book of fate
And there the last assizes keep,
For those who wake and those who sleep :

When rattling bones together fly,
From the four corners of the sky ;
When sinews o'er the skeletons are spread,
Those clothed with flesh, and life inspires the dead ;
The sacred poets first shall hear the sound,
And foremost from the tomb shall bound,
For they are covered with the lightest ground ;
And straight, with inborn vigour, on the wing,
Like mounting larks, to the new morning sing.
There thou, sweet saint ! before the choir shall go,
As harbinger of heaven, the way to show,
The way which thou so well has learnt below.

In the register her burial is dated 15th April
1685, the entry being very brief, " Mad^m· Anne
Killegrew, Dau^r· of Doctor Killegrew." She is
not to be confounded with her aunt, another
Anne Killegrew, the first wife of George Kirk,
who was also beautiful, also celebrated in contemporary poetry, and who was more unfortunate in her death, for she was drowned by
an accident in the Thames while shooting the
rapids at London Bridge in 1641.

The monument stood on the eastern side of
the chapel, not far from the vestry door and
the pulpit. Her mother, who seems to have
been the first wife of Dr. Killegrew, died in
1682, and was also buried here, as were two
other members of the family in 1695, and a
third, Charles, in 1725.

In this year also, March 12, 1725, there is

a record of the burial of " Alexander Pendarvis, Esq." He was not a poet or anything approaching it, but has a place in literature nevertheless, as the first husband of the celebrated Mary Granville, Mrs. Delany, whose delightful memoirs were published by Lady Llanover in 1861. Mr. Pendarvis was M.P. for Launceston. Lady Llanover seems to be in doubt as to the exact date of his death, but places it, with a query, in 1724. The above entry, now first printed, sets the question at rest.

Poets of the Savoy. Mr. Pendarvis.

CHAPTER XIV.

𝔗𝔥𝔢 ℭ𝔥𝔞𝔭𝔢𝔩 𝔦𝔫 𝔈𝔠𝔩𝔦𝔭𝔰𝔢.

The Savoy marriages—John Wilkinson—Eleven hundred weddings—An advertisement—Mr. Wilkinson's refusal to marry the lady's-maid—A pluralist—Archibald Cameron's death.

AFTER the suppression of the hospital and the removal of the parishioners of St. Mary le Strand to their new church, a period of comparative eclipse comes over the fortunes of our chapel; an eclipse which, however, as in the case of the sun and moon, was much observed by the general public. The scandals caused by what were called Fleet marriages, brought upon the Savoy a very unpleasant share of notice, and only a stern sense of duty enables the unwilling historian to record the events of Mr. Wilkinson's incumbency. They are fully detailed in the late John Southerden Burn's curious volume on *The Fleet Registers*, and as I have nothing to add to what he has recorded, and as his book is somewhat scarce, I venture to extract the whole passage as it stands :—

"Although the Savoy was one of those places with pretended privileges, there do not appear to have been any clandestine marriages there until after the passing of the Marriage Act ; the number of marriages for a few years before and after that period being as follows :—

1752	.	. .	15
1753	.	. .	19
1754	.	. .	342
1755	.	. .	1190
1756	.	. .	63
1757	.	. .	13
1758	.	. .	17

On the passing of the Marriage Act, the Rev. John Wilkinson began to exercise his supposed rights as Minister of the Savoy, considering himself authorised to grant licenses as a privilege annexed to the Savoy, as being extra-parochial, and because Dr. Killegrew and others of his predecessors had granted them. The Savoy, therefore, soon became known as a place for easy matrimony, and his marriages brought him 'a profusion of cash, and instead of thinking of a rainy day, all was rat-tat-tat at the street door, and a variety of company. Easter-day was crowded from eight till twelve. So many pairs were for the indissoluble knot being tied, that he might have made a fortune had he been blessed with patience and prudence, and been contented with publishing the banns of marriage only. Many persons came out of curiosity to hear such a long list of spinsters announced.'*

"Mr. Wilkinson had hints from Government of the consequences of these practices, and at length, proceedings were taken against him; and he was accustomed to make his escape over the leads at the Savoy, through the kitchen of the prison (which was then there) to a private door into the chapel, to evade those who were set to watch him.

"One Sunday morning an alarm was given that the officers were in the church; a general panic ensued in his family; he sent word that he was suddenly taken ill, and could not read prayers, and made his way down the garden to a gate that opened on the Thames, reached Somerset Stairs, where he took a boat and got into Kent. Having arrived there, he engaged Mr. Grierson to perform the marriages as his curate; but the licenses he granted himself, thinking that Mr. Grierson could not suffer for what he, in his authority as Minister of the Savoy, was to be responsible for.

"Very shortly after this, Mr. Vernon of

* Tate Wilkinson's *Memoirs*.

Drury Lane Theatre, was married by Mr. Grierson to Miss Portier. Garrick insisted on seeing the certificate, which Mr. Vernon obtained from Mr. Grierson and gave to Garrick, who handed it over to Mr. Carrington, the King's Messenger. Mr. Grierson was thereupon taken up and tried for having married the parties; was convicted and transported for fourteen years. In his defence, he said he was not aware of the illegality of the marrying at the Savoy, as he had married his own son there.

"After the committal of Mr. Grierson, Mr. Wilkinson engaged the Rev. Mr. Brooks as his curate, and continued to derive great profits from his marriages. Considering himself certain of an acquittal, he determined to surrender himself and take his trial, which he accordingly did on the 11th July 1756: he was tried on the 16th; convicted, and sentenced to fourteen years transportation. The vessel which was to take him to America sailed early in March 1757, but by stress of weather was driven to Plymouth, where Mr. Wilkinson died from an attack of the gout. His widow died in 1763; he left an only child, Tate Wilkinson, the comedian."

It was during this miserable period that the celebrated advertisement appeared in the papers, setting forth the advantages of the Savoy for

The Chapel in eclipse.

marriages, as having "five private ways by land, and two by water,"* the expense to be "not more than one guinea, the five-shilling stamp included."

Here I would very willingly close my account of the Reverend Mr. Wilkinson. But a discovery made by Mr. Martin among the Winchilsea papers, recently added to the collection in the British Museum, is too curious to be omitted. A letter not addressed contains the following passage :—†

Mr. Wilkinson's refusal to marry the lady's-maid.

"My Lord—Howsoever some people may sink beneath their characters by reporting things entirely false and groundless, I cannot say ; but, My Lord, I cou'd not be easy untill I had solemnly assured your Grace that the late Earl of Winchilsea gave me the presentations in every respect truly great and noble ; and that a wife was never whispered to me till the day after my Lord's Death : then indeed, my Lady Herself told me that her maid Morffee was always intended to go along with the Livings, and that if I desired to make Her Ladysp. my Friend, I must not refuse the Offer : I own, my Lord, I was at first unable to give a direct answer, but recovering the

* *Public Advertiser*, Jan. 2, 1754.

† Add. MS., 29,549, f. 129. This letter was printed in the *Pall Mall Gazette*, in October 1874, but I had at that time no suspicion that John Wilkinson was the notorious minister of the Savoy.

surprise, I gave Her Ladysp. an absolute denial, *The Chapel in eclipse.* upon wch she in a passion ordered me to withdraw, and I have never seen Her Ladysp. since."

This strange document is dated Nov. 3, 1729. There are some further particulars of no moment in it. On turning to a note in Mr. Burn's book, I find that John Wilkinson described himself as " His Majesty's Chaplain of the Savoy, Chaplain to His late Royal Highness, Frederick, Prince of Wales, Rector of Eastwell, Kent, and Curate of Wye." Eastwell Rectory and the perpetual curacy of Wye were both in the gift of Lord Winchilsea, and are, of course, the livings mentioned in the letter. According to Hasted, Wilkinson was presented to Wye in 1729, and to Eastwell on the 26th May 1730, and resigned the latter incumbency in 1733. Mr. Burn adds that " in 1732 he is described as rector of Coyley, in the county of Glamorgan, and stipendiary curate of Wye," and that he was " educated at St. Bees in Cornwall (query, Cumberland?) and finished his studies at Oxford." In 1743 Heneage Dering was presented to Wye, so that Wilkinson seems to have held it for ten years longer than Eastwell. A John Wilkinson of Queen's College, who took the degree of B.A. at Oxford in 1723, may be the same person.*

A pluralist.

---

* In the Record Office there remains a manuscript

As to the "Maid Morffee," she does not
seem to have secured him for a husband, in
spite of Lady Winchilsea's efforts on her behalf,
for Wilkinson was married in the Savoy, on 26th
April 1731, to Grace, daughter of Alderman
Tate, of Carlisle. His son, mentioned above,
was the celebrated actor, Tate Wilkinson, whose
amusing *Memoirs* were published in 1790.

It was during Wilkinson's incumbency that a
tragical event, commemorated in one of the
windows to be described farther on, took place.
Among the number of the rebel army defeated
at Culloden was Archibald Cameron,* a medical
man, third son of John Cameron of Lochiel.
In the battle he succoured indifferently both
friends and foes, ministering to the wounded of
both parties. Finding himself proscribed, he
fled to the Low Countries, where old Lochiel
was then living. But in 1753 he was so imprudent as to return to Scotland, owing, as he
said afterwards, to an inclination to see some
friends. "At a place called Lochlommond in
his way to Lochaber," he was seen, identified,
and betrayed by a person who watched him into

entitled a *History of the Royal Hospital of the Savoy from
1260 to Michaelmas 1755.* It was written by Wilkinson
with the idea of making himself out the lawful successor
of the Masters.

* Called Charles Archibald Cameron in the *Gentleman's Magazine,* 1753.

a house. He made no resistance, and was taken first to Stirling and thence to Edinburgh by a party of dragoons. On the 10th April he started with a strong escort for London, which he reached on the 19th, and was lodged in the Tower. His trial was brief. Though at first he endeavoured to raise a question of identification, he soon submitted, behaving, according to a contemporary report,* with decency and composure, and pleading the various acts of humanity and kindness which he had performed to mitigate the horrors of the rebellion. Glasgow, he said, and apparently without contradiction, would probably have been burnt by the insurgents but for his mediation. But nothing he said availed him. In the eye of the law he was guilty, and his judges had no choice but to pronounce upon him the horrible doom in force against high treason. He heard them with a remarkable composure. There was, we read, no alteration of countenance, "except that his lips closed and his mouth began to fill." He went from the bar with three or four low reverences to the bench, against whose sentence he does not seem to have uttered a complaint, either then or afterwards. Strange to say, no effort seems to have been made to obtain a pardon from the Crown.

* *Gent. Mag.* as above.

The Chapel in eclipse.

In the Tower his behaviour was equally marked by calmness, courage, and resignation. It was such, says our authority, "as became his unhappy circumstances, manly and sedate." He was denied the use of pen and ink except in the presence of his gaolors, and made some notes with a blunt pencil on scraps of paper, in which he defended his conduct and political creed, but the defence has never, that I am aware, been published. He gave these notes to his wife, from whom he was parted on the evening before the fatal day. He asked for her again the next morning, but she had already gone away.

On Thursday, 7th June, while the King, George II., was occupied at . Westminster in proroguing Parliament, while the streets were full of loyal acclamations, and the tranquil state of the realm, and especially of the lately rebellious Scotland, was subject of universal congratulation, a sad procession moved from the Tower, through the city, past Newgate, down the hill, and up again to Oxford Street, then but lately named, and so, past the stately new mansions of Cavendish Square and Bond Street, to the bare heath at the corner where Tyburn Lane became the Edgeware Road. Everywhere anxious faces were to be seen. Vast crowds, in spite of the rival procession, were assembled.

It was a common sight to see the king open Parliament, or half-a-dozen wretches hanging round a triangle; but it would be something new to see a man quartered. Shenstone's ballad was but too fresh in men's ears, its scene but too familiar to their eyes, though it was now a long time since the next previous execution of a rebel. Besides mere curiosity, not a few, it seems, had come to see the last of an old friend, and Dr. Cameron saluted politely many whom he recognised. Long and fatiguing such a drive must have been on a sledge, over rough roads and through miry ruts; where, even with well-hung carriages and wood pavement, it is more than sufficiently tiring. Two hours and a quarter were consumed on the road to Tyburn; and when at length he arrived under the gallows he expressed himself as fatigued, indeed, but not in any way unnerved. His deportment is described as heroic. He stepped lightly into the hangman's cart; and apologising politely for keeping any one waiting a moment, he remarked cheerfully to the chaplain that he looked on this as his second birth-day, adding, with a smile, that there had not been so many people present at the first. After a brief conversation with the sheriff, he turned to the chaplain, whose name is not given, and told him he had done with the world, and was glad to leave it; expressed himself a loyal and steadfast but unworthy member of the Church of England, and bade him farewell. As the clergyman descended from the cart his foot slipped, and Cameron, with a spirit which reminds us of one of the older heroes of the scaffold—of More or of Raleigh—cried out, "Have a care, sir ; you know not this way so well as I do."

These were his last words : after hanging, by the special humanity of the officials, for twenty minutes, he was cut down, his body cut open, and his heart—that heart which had been always tender to others' suffering, but which had not failed him in courage at the supreme moment— was consumed in the fire prepared for it. The quartering was omitted, and all the other insults to which the body of Shenstone's rebel had been exposed. . On the following Sunday, 10th June, his remains were laid "in the large vault in the Savoy Chapel."

A hundred years later the clement councils of Queen Victoria permitted the erection of a beautiful monument to Cameron in the Chapel. It was exhibited previously at the Royal Academy, where it attracted some notice, not only from its own merits, but because of the melancholy interest attaching to the story here condensed. This memorial, put up by the Scottish hero's grandson, was lost, like so many others, in the fire of 1864, and a window has

taken its place. Archibald Cameron was the
last who suffered death for the cause of the
young Pretender.

THE CHAPEL TOWER IN 1787.

CHAPTER XV.

𝕿𝖍𝖊 𝕮𝖍𝖆𝖕𝖊𝖑 𝕽𝖔𝖞𝖆𝖑.

The Chapel is made Royal—The Ministers or Chaplains from 1773 to 1859—The church improved—The barrel organ banished—The pulpit—The hour-glass —The monuments—The Chapel burnt—Rebuilt and opened—The two first Preachers.

THE subsequent history of the Chapel is soon told. After Wilkinson's departure, but how, I know not, William Wilmot became minister.* He made his first entry in the Register on the 26th September 1756. He had been here seventeen years when George III. (on the 27th November 1773), issued a patent constituting the church a Chapel Royal, and appointing Mr. Wilmot " chaplain, or minister, during pleasure."

* For this part of the story I am indebted to the notes of the Rev. Robert Gwynne, vicar of St. Mary, Soho, who, while curate of St. Mary le Strand, published brief but very complete accounts of St. Mary's and of the Savoy in the *Church Chronicle*, June and July 1869, under the editorship of Mr. Charles Mackeson.

Mr. Wilmot, thus recognised, continued to serve here until the spring of 1778. After his death his place does not seem to have been immediately filled, and a number of temporary ministers appear in the book, among them Samuel Ayscough, a well known antiquary and bibliographer, whose labours as Assistant Librarian at the British Museum, in its infancy, are not yet forgotten. His name occurs five times in 1784. James Hodgson was appointed 19th August 1795. On the 25th March 1805, Dr. John Banks Jenkinson, afterwards Bishop of St. David's, was appointed. He was a brother of Lord Liverpool, and became prebendary of Worcester three years later, and dean of the same cathedral in 1818. These preferments he held with the Savoy. On the 24th June 1825, immediately after Dr. Jenkinson's promotion to the bench, Andrew Brandram was appointed chaplain. Of him I know nothing more. In 1838 (3d Dec.), he was succeeded by John Foster, who was appointed to the rectory of Stambourne, Essex, in 1858, and did not immediately resign the Savoy, a curate being placed in charge for a few months. Ultimately, on Whitsunday 1859, Henry White came into the office, which he still holds, and to which that of Chaplain in Ordinary to the Queen has been added.

The Chapel Royal.
The church improved.

During the incumbency of Mr. Foster some very sweeping changes, for the most part to be reckoned improvements, were carried out at the expense of her Majesty. The pews, which had been of what is known as the "pen" order, were made single. The destroyed portion of the reredos was replaced, and the window above it opened. The entrance to Savoy Hill was closed, and the present chief entrance made through the churchyard. In 1860 the gallery was removed and other improvements effected under the care of Mr. Smirke, R.A. At the same time a careful cleansing and renovation was bestowed upon the ceiling.

The barrel organ banished.

It was at the earlier period that the old pair of barrel organs which had long done duty in the chapel was taken away, and its place supplied with a more worthy instrument.

The pulpit.

The hourglass.

In the pulpit stood an hour-glass, somewhat resembling that which still remains at St. Albans, Wood Street, and in a few other churches. The pulpit itself was shifted in 1860.

The monuments.

Of the monuments which blocked up the chancel and were dotted here and there all over the walls at both sides, I am able, though almost all have perished, to offer a very full account. Some were wholly or in part concealed by the pews. Some had decayed and fallen from their places. Some had become illegible.

Some had disappeared altogether. But at the period of which I am writing a very large number still remained, and as records exist of the epitaphs upon fifty or more, I will endeavour to point out the most interesting, merely naming the rest.

About a hundred and fifty years ago a careful and industrious antiquary, John Strype, made a copy of all the inscriptions he could see. His list comprises forty different memorials.*

In the north-east angle of the chapel was a tablet inscribed : " Here lieth Nazareth Coppin, wife to George Coppin of London, gentleman, daughter to Thomas Thwaits of Hardington, in the county of Norfolk, gentleman, who being of the age of twenty-four years, in the prime of her youth and beauty, as she lived most virtuously, so she died most godly the 22d of June 1592, in the 34th year of the most happy reign of Queen Elizabeth. Mors certa, inevitabilis, incerta."

Below this was the tablet of " Mrs. Anne Killegrew."

Opposite, on the west side, a black marble slab to Sir Richard Rokeby and Jane his wife. She died on the 15th and he on the 27th April

* Stowe's *Survey of the Cities of London and West-minster;* corrected and enlarged by John Strype in 1720; sixth edition, 1754.

1523. Perhaps, like the bishops buried here the year before, they died of the plague. The tomb is figured by J. T. Smith, as "an antient monument in the chancel of St. Mary le Savoy."

Against the reredos on the west side was a tomb with the effigy of Sir Robert Douglas and his wife Nichola Moray. The epitaph, which was written by "Da. Humius," referred to the lady only, and was very long, and in Latin. She died in November 1612. I shall have occasion, in the next chapter, to record the preservation of her little kneeling statue.

Over the vestry door a "fair tomb" to Alicia, daughter to Simon Steward, of Kingeth in Suffolk. She died 18th June 1573. There is an engraving of this monument also in Smith's *London*.

On a stone in the chancel the name of Peter Lilly, D.D., a brother of the Savoy, who died 1st June 1627, and of his daughter, Mary, who died in 1625. Near it was a monument to Francis Bulbeck of Clevedon, Somerset, who died unmarried in 1585. According to an entry in the register, 24th August 1684, the body of Elizabeth Jennyns, daughter of Sir John Jennyns and Dorothy his wife, the heiress of the Bulbecks, was buried under the same monument.

Close by were also monuments to Peter

Richardson, goldsmith to Henry VIII. and his three successors, 1586; to David Bedo, steward to Lord Carlisle, 1541; to Humphrey Lovel, 1585, his two wives and five children; to Richard Ellis, "Hospitularius," 1550; and, in the east corner of the chancel, to William Chaworth, 2d son of John Chaworth of Wynnerton, Notts, who died in 1582, aged 28. The next is called by Strype "a very fair table with rich coat of arms." It commemorated Rebecca, the wife of Captain Nicholas Burton, and daughter of Henry Somaster of Painsford in Devonshire, who died in 1632.

On the wall at the west side of the church was the monument of Summerset already mentioned.* Next to it that of William Vevian, son and heir of Michael Vevian of Cornwall, "by misfortune drowned in the Thames on Passion Sunday at afternoon, in the year of our Lord God 1520." Here were also the tablets of Humphrey Gosling, John Floid, John Sampull, and Humphrey Cook, described already.†

On the south (west) side of the communion-table was a small kneeling figure, in a niche of the tabernacle work of the reredos, representing Joyce, daughter of Sir Alan Apsley, Lieutenant of the Tower, and sister of the famous Lucy Hutchinson. She was widow of Lyster Blunt,

* See p. 165. † See pp. 166, 167.

The Chapel Royal

and of William, Earl of Dalhousie, and died in 1663.

Strype also mentions memorials of the sixteenth century to George Skoowith (?), 1525; John Dangon, 1577; Eleanor Kempe, 1559; Anna Pynta, a Spaniard, 1523; John Baine, "Sacerdos," 1525; John Borwet, 1525; Newel Loveday, 1523; and of the seventeenth to Elizabeth Compton, daughter of Lord Compton, an infant, 1629; and her sister Lady Mary, born after their father had become Earl of Northampton, 1634; to Arabella, Countess of Nottingham, 1681; Anne Comberford, 1663; Samuel Howe, 1670; Magdalene Lane, 1684; Sir Richard Blake, 1683; Sir William Howard, 1672; Edward, Lord Howard of Escrick, 1675; and Charles Fitzpatrick, 1677.

There were also some later monuments. One to John Hewet, 1705; a second to Robert Brown, 1709; a third to Robert Burch, 1789.

In a book * which I cannot consider a trustworthy source of information, I find the following vague note :— " In the chapel was a monument, rather sumptuous, erected about 1715 in honour of a merchant; the sole statement of the epitaph was that he had bequeathed £5

---

* *Curiosities of London*, by John Timbs, p. 143. Mr. Timbs, as usual, omitted the reference to the authority from which he quoted this account.

to the poor of the Savoy precinct and a like sum to the poor of the parish of St. Mary le Strand; while at the side, and occupying about half the breadth of the marble, the money was expressed in figures, just as in a page of a ledger, with lines single and double, perpendicular, and, at the bottom, horizontal; the whole being summed up, and in each line two cyphers for shillings and one for pence. The epitaph concluded, 'which sum was duly paid by his executors.'"

We have now but three of these old monuments; namely, the brass plate to Bishops Halsey and Douglas; the little figure of Alice Steward, being but a fragment of her whole cenotaph; and the statuette, in a mutilated condition, of Lady Douglas.

In 1834 a tablet was erected to the memory of Richard Lander, the African traveller. For it is now substituted a stained glass window, described farther on.

In 1843 the newly-opened window over the reredos was filled with stained glass. The parishioners, desirous of marking their sense of the royal bounty by which the chapel was made so much more commodious, subscribed and commissioned Mr. Willement to design the glass. It bore this inscription." This window was glazed at the cost of the congregation, in honour of God and in gratitude to our Queen Victoria."

At the same time considerable interest was excited among antiquaries by the cleaning and restoration of the painted roof. It was thus described by Mr. Lockhart* at the time :—

"The ceiling resembles the nearly contemporary one of the chapel at St. James's Palace, being wholly of wood (oak and pear tree), flat, with a slight core next the walls ; but, instead of the angular panels which cover the whole surface of the Chapel Royal, with the initials H. A. painted on them, the roof in the Savoy is divided by moulded ribs into one hundred and thirty-eight quatrefoil panels, each enriched with a carved ornament, either of sacred or of historical significance. The panels number twenty-three in the length of the chapel, and six in its width. The ten ranges, commencing at the north window, and extending considerably to the southward of the altar steps, have each in its centre a shield surrounded by the crown of thorns, each shield presenting, in high relief, some feature or emblem of the passion and death of our Lord ; and all devised and arranged in a style of which we have many examples in sacred buildings of the fifteenth and

* *Notice of the Savoy Chapel,* 1844, printed by command of Her Majesty for private circulation.

sixteenth centuries. In one quatrefoil are the garments and the dice; in another the cross; in a third the sponge and the spear; in a fourth is the head of the high priest's servant with the sword of Peter behind his ear. Elsewhere we see a halbert and a lanthorn; the column and scourge; a torch and cresset; the salutation of Judas; heads of Peter and Pilate's servant; the cock; the heads of Pilate and Caiaphas; the five wounds on a heart, two hands, and two feet; a pelican; an open sepulchre with three pots of myrrh. The exterior panels have angels supporting the cross, the ladder, the spear, the crown of thorns, the napkin of St. Veronica, and the column of the scourging. The panels throughout the rest of the ceiling are occupied by bearings or badges, indicating the various families from which the royal lineage was derived, more particularly the alliances of the House of Lancaster; each of these panels being surrounded in place of the crown of thorns towards the altar end, with a torch or wreath tinted with the livery colours of the various families, respectively. Thus, we have the Red Dragon of Cadwallader; the Black Bull of Clare; the White Hart of Richard II.; the White Hind of his mother, the Fair Maid of Kent; The White Falcon of York; the White Lion of March; the Antelope of Henry V.; the Winged

Stag of France; the Golden Lion, regally crowned, of England; the White Greyhound of Henry VII.; the Antelope and Ibex, with curved horns and spotted skin, being the badge or 'best' of Margaret of Richmond, mother to that king, the same that is displayed so frequently on her Colleges at Cambridge : and in many of the smaller compartments, what has already been alluded to as marking the date of the decoration, the pomegranate of Catherine of Arragon, a badge first adopted by her father on the surrender of Granada in 1491."

The reredos has been alluded to more than once. It has been attributed to Sir Reginald Bray, the architect of St. George's Chapel, at Windsor, but I fear the dates will hardly suit, for Sir Reginald died in 1503. A very careful survey was made of it by James Peller Malcolm at the beginning of this century. He says that on the east side of the window a considerable fragment then remained, from which the appearance of the whole might be judged. It consisted of a double panel on each side of a niche, which terminated originally in delicate pinnacles. "The niches are separated by quatrefoils, each leaf of which is filled with trefoils, and the centres by the rose in one, and portcullis in the other. The canopy of the niche has six sides in the lower and three in the upper divisions, separated

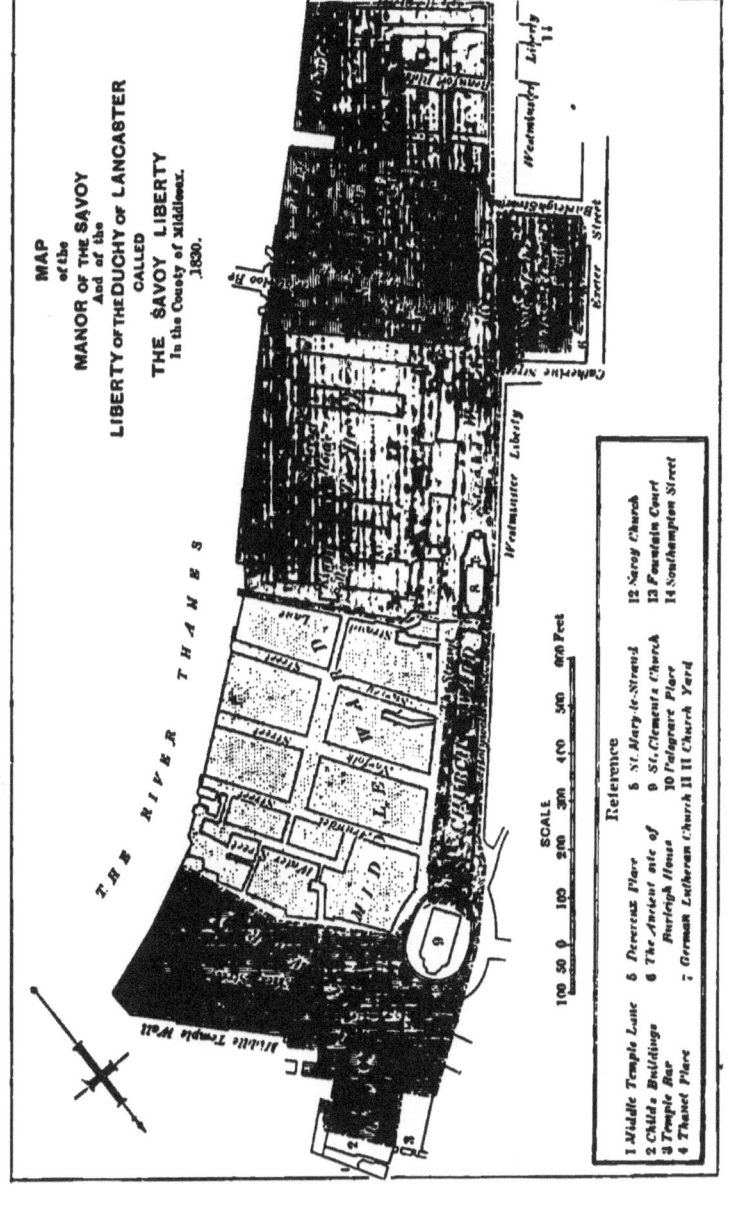

MAP
of the
MANOR OF THE SAVOY
And of the
LIBERTY OF THE DUCHY OF LANCASTER
CALLED
THE SAVOY LIBERTY
In the County of Middlesex.
1830.

SCALE

100 50 0   100   200   300   400   500   600 Feet

Reference

1 Middle Temple Lane   5 Devereux Place   8 St. Mary-le-Strand   12 Savoy Church
2 Child's Buildings   6 The Ancient site of   9 St. Clement's Church   13 Fountain Court
3 Temple Bar   Burleigh House   10 Palsgrave Place   14 Southampton Street
4 Thanet Place   7 German Lutheran Church 11 11 Church Yard

by the pinnacles of the cinquefoil arches. Each side is pierced into beautiful little windows, and the whole terminates in a dome of quatrefoils, surmounted by a pinnacle." The corresponding portion on the west side was obliterated by monuments, among them, as we have already seen, the figure of Lady Douglas.

There was also some fine panelling in the church, the walls being originally wainscoted up to eight feet from the ground. Much of it had perished before the fatal fire, when, of course, the rest was consumed. On the front of the gallery, which had occupied the southern end, were formerly twelve panels painted with figures of the Apostles, and other similar representations were at either side of the chancel window.

Such then was the Chapel Royal when, on the afternoon of Thursday the 7th July, 1864, a fire broke out which entirely destroyed all the fittings, the roof, and the monuments, not sparing the restored reredos, or Mr. Willement's fine window. Indeed, it seems to have raged with double fury at that end of the church, for the two houses in the Strand which most nearly adjoined were burnt out. It began at an hour when no one was in the church; and has been attributed to some flaw in the warming apparatus. The very next day Lord Clarendon informed the Chaplain and congregation that her Majesty had commanded the restoration of the chapel, and on the Advent Sunday of 1865 (Dec. 3) it was once more opened for divine worship. The restoration, which was conducted wholly at the cost of her Majesty, involved an expenditure of about £7000, Mr. Smirke being the architect.

The opening day was one of sincere rejoicing and thankfulness. Though the great company of witnesses which had looked down from the old walls before the fire, was now gone, yet to many of those present even the walls were sacred, and every stone eloquent. The temple purged by fire was even more glorious than before in their eyes. Dean Stanley preached a sermon in which were mingled with happy art the present congratulations and the old associations. His text, " Gather up the fragments that remain, that nothing be lost" (St. John, vi. 12), was admirably suited to the occasion. The evening congregation was addressed by Frederick Denison Maurice, whose impressive voice none who once heard it can ever forget. He never preached again at the Savoy, and before very long was gathered to that rest which he had so well earned. The present writer, who was more than most men indebted to his kindly ministration, rejoices exceedingly to be able to include his among the sacred memories of the Savoy.

CHAPTER XVI.

𝕿𝖍𝖊 𝕮𝖍𝖆𝖕𝖊𝖑 𝖆𝖘 𝖎𝖙 𝖎𝖘.

Charles Dickens's account of it—Three exterior inscriptions—The interior dimensions—The font—The pulpit — Rescued monuments — The roof — The Prince Consort at the Savoy—The Windows.

THE pleasant aspect of the precinct, even before the recent clearing of dilapidated buildings and the migration of the German Chapel, has been celebrated by so many writers that I will only allude to it in passing, while I quote the words of no less an authority than the late Charles Dickens, who thus described it :*—" If you would view the outside, look upon it at early morning, ere the working smoke has poisoned and obscured the air—ere that hot, damp, dusty day-cloud has arisen man's stature high : the cloud that to me is always rife in London streets, and whose presence I ascribe to the perpetual trampling of men's feet seeking gold or glory.

* In *All the Year Round.*

The Chapel as it is. At early morn there is not a quoin in the old Chapel wall, not a mullion in its blinking windows, not a cartouch or a cantaliver, but stands forth sharp and clear in its proper light, shade, and reflection, as in a Venetian photograph. You shall see the rugosities of the stone as through an opera-glass; you shall count the strands in the cordage of the rigging of the great hay-boats floating up or down the river. This early morning beautifies and enriches everything. As Sydney Smith used to bid his little servant-maid draw up the window-blinds on a sunshiny morning, and 'glorify the room,' so does the summer sun glorify the hoar old Precinct, and render lovely the ugly modern 'improvements' in bricks and boarding. Even the sullen wreaths of smoke that will rise—all Smoke-prevention Acts notwithstanding—and accumulate in wreaths and ridges from kilns and furnaces never quenched, in far-off Bermondsey or remote South Lambeth, even this indomitable murk turns golden and cream-coloured when Aurora touches it with her finger-tips. Away, the clock-tower of Westminster Palace rises, not like a kitchen clock—the guise it wears when you survey it from Bridge-street—but pale pink, shaded and fretted blue, and glittering with golden shafts. At early morn you can discern the dots that mark the minutes from numeral to numeral, on the dial. As for the trees and grass in the Chapel garden—they thrive wondrously for London vegetation, and gather no smoke—they can scarcely be said to be green at early morn. The leaves and herbage seem chameleon-hued. You shall find maize and primrose in their lights, blue and purple in their shadows. Laminæ of silver play on blades and veins; and, upon my word, I think that on summer nights the dew falls here —the only dew that is shed in all London, beyond the tears of the homeless."

He thus concludes :—

"So run the sands of life through this quiet hour-glass. So glides the Life away in the old Precinct. At its base, a river runs for all the world; at its summit, is the brawling, raging Strand; on either side, are the gloomy Adelphi Arches, the Bridge of Sighs, that men call Waterloo. But the Precinct troubles itself little with the noise and tumult, and sleeps well through life, without its fitful fever."

If we have come to see the chapel, however, we must not allow any of these feelings to delay us, for there is much to be done. Let us take the exterior first. Three inscriptions will engage our attention. There is behind the chapel a narrow street known as Savoy Hill. At its Strand end is the "little gate," often mentioned, approached by a steep flight of steps.   At the other end was formerly the beautiful oriel (shown* below of the barracks and prison,

THE CHAPEL AND PRISON IN THE 18TH CENTURY.

burnt in 1776.   On the left hand was and is the chapel, a doorway now built up leading directly into the chancel.   Over this door we read on a classical tablet :—" This chapel was repaired and improved at the expense of His Majesty King George the Fourth in the years 1826 and 1830."

* By the kind liberality of the S.P.C.K.

Returning past the great chancel window, to the "chapel garth," by Church Row, we enter by a gate at the north-east corner. The ground is full of green grass and trees, and it is not till we approach very close that we can read, on a handsome tablet ornamented with regal ensigns, the words :—" The interior of this chapel was improved and restored at the cost of Her Majesty Queen Victoria, A.D. MDCCCXLIII." This tablet is now partly hidden by the roof of the new Vestry, but it records work wholly obliterated by the fire in 1864, as we shall presently see.

Proceeding now to the southern end of the chapel, we observe as we descend a flight of steps to the principal entrance a third tablet of a very different character, yet of peculiar interest. "Thomas Britton died November 12th 1839, aged 101 years." Beyond his reluctance in leaving it, here recorded, Thomas Britton seems to have made no mark on this world.

There are two mural tablets near the vestry, and the whole garden is studded with tombs and little monuments, among which we need only single out for notice that which marks the last resting-place of William Hilton, R.A., the painter, who died in 1839; it consists of a small but handsome cross.

Entering the chapel at the lower end we are

The Chapel as it is.

The interior dimensions.

struck at once by the great simplicity of its aspect, a simplicity made only the more obvious by the magnificence of the decorations. It is, in fact, a single rectangular chamber, without any architectural features to break its length of 89 feet 2 inches, except that two windows on either side at the northern or chancel end, are slightly smaller than the six which light the southern end or nave. It is 23 feet 9 inches in width throughout, and the altar is raised by a gradual ascent of five steps, the first of which is thirty feet from the reredos which, restored from the fragments of the old reredos already described, is of great beauty and intricacy of design. Before entering the chancel, we pause

The font.

to observe, facing the entrance door, the font, which is in a style harmonising with the reredos ; it was designed by Mr. Blore, and behind it is a tablet bearing this inscription :—" This font was presented to the Chapel Royal of the Savoy by Harriet de Wint in place of a Monument previously erected to the memory of her brother, William Hilton, R.A., her husband, Peter de Wint, and other members of her family, whose remains are interred in the adjoining cemetery. The Monument was destroyed by the fire, July VII. MDCCCLXIV. May this tribute of earthly affection be long preserved to the glory of God." It will be seen that the inscription commemorates a second painter, Peter de Wint, whose works have increased constantly in public estimation since his death. Close to the tablet on the right is a curious little "gold ground" picture of the Holy Family, probably of the early Siennese school; it seems to be one of those mentioned as being in the Master's lodgings at the dissolution,* and having been sold or stolen, found its way to Hereford, whither it was traced by Mr. White in 1876 and restored to the Savoy.

Reserving our notice of the windows for the moment, we proceed towards the chancel. The pulpit stands on the right beside the new doorway opened in 1877, and at the first step. It is of carved oak, on a stone base, and bears an hour-glass, imitated from that which was destroyed in the fire. Above it on the wall is this inscription :—"To the glory of God and the gospel of Jesus Christ this pulpit was dedicated in sacred memory of John Burgess, who died April 24, 1820, aged 70, and of William Robert Burgess, who died May 8, 1853, aged 74."

The stalls for the choir are on either side behind the pulpit, and a doorway in the east wall leads into the new vestry.† Beyond this door and within the rails, is a very beautiful

* See p. 158.   † See p. 224.

*The Chapel
as it is.*

Rescued
monuments.
double niche for Sedilia. Beyond it in the
corner is a small piscina, much worn, which
having been blocked up by a monument was
brought to light after the fire. On the wall,
near the door, on a neat stone bracket, one of
the two kneeling figures preserved from among
the old monuments has lately been replaced.
It is probably that of Alice Steward, and if so
was originally over the vestry door, and bore
in the folded hands a skull.

The description of the old reredos will answer
equally for the present one, to which not long
ago stone statues of St. Peter and St. Paul were
added.

In the centre of the chancel, not far from the
lower step of the altar, is a black slab bearing
the brass already described,* of Bishop Halsey
and Bishop Douglas, whose bodies rest below.
This, the most interesting of our monuments,
attracts many visitors, especially from beyond
the Tweed. It is intended shortly to replace
on the western wall the effigy of another personage of the Douglas name. The statue of Sir
Robert Douglas, behind which that of his wife
knelt, was crumbled into dust by the fire. The

* Erected in 1877 from the designs of Messrs. Perry
and Reed: a very handsome room which the visitor should
see, with its armorial shields and windows, and the fine
open timber roof.

smaller figure was long lost, and has only been restored to the chapel within a few weeks by the last of a long chapter of accidents which led to its discovery and identification. Is it too much to hope that some other fragments, hidden like this one, in private collections, may yet be brought home to the Chapel Royal? Elsewhere they are probably not even ornamental. Here they are of the highest value and interest.

The Chapel as it is.

The mural decorations and the roof next claim our attention. The old carved and painted ceiling having perished, it was found impossible for many reasons to restore it, except in the general features of the design. The new roof is magnificently coloured, but with less elaborate devices than at first. It contains within quatrefoils a series of shields of the royal persons who have been connected with the manor, terminating with the arms of her Majesty and those of the lamented Prince Consort, of whom, in some sense, the restoration is intended as a memorial.* Immediately

The roof.

---

* The shields are fourteen in number. 1. Peter of Savoy. 2. John of France. 3. Henry III. 4. Edmund of Lancaster. 5. Henry of Lancaster. 6. Henry Duke of Lancaster. 7. John of Gaunt. 8. Henry IV. 9. Henry VI. 10. Edward IV. 11. Henry VII. 12. Henry VIII. 13. Queen Victoria. 14. The Prince Consort.

The Chapel as it is.

The Prince Consort at the Savoy.

after the former restoration in 1844, his Royal Highness visited the precinct and the little chapel, and here, twenty years after, his arms, his badge and crest, and his initials were painted as a remembrance of him. Immediately over the communion-table these memorials, sacred as they are to the subjects of the Queen, are succeeded by others still more sacred. The "pelican in her piety," the lamb and banner of the Baptist, to whom the chapel is dedicated, the cross, the spear, the monogram, and other holy emblems are depicted in delicate colours. At the top of the wall, where the roof is slightly arched, are angelic figures, each bearing on a shield, as in the old roof, one of the implements of the Passion. Here is the purple robe, near it the money bag marked xxx; then the three nails, the dice, the sponge, and the crown of thorns. The lower part of the chancel wall is decorated only with diapers, in which gold is harmoniously mingled with crimson and red and white; while below the first step of the sanctuary a less gorgeous but not less effective pattern is used.

The windows.

Now we turn to the windows, which perhaps we should have taken first, as they will probably strike the eye of the visitor before anything else. The great window over the holy table has succeeded one which the inhabitants of the precinct put up, as already mentioned, in gratitude to the Queen for the improvements effected in the Chapel The new window records their mourning at the premature loss of the Prince Consort, and was, we believe, the last work undertaken by the venerable artist, Thomas Willement, by whom the former glass had been executed. His eye had not dimmed, nor the force of his colour abated, and the result, though not quite in accord with the later windows which adorn the chapel, is eminently pleasing. The design is full of tender feeling. By the cross of the Redeemer stand the Virgin Mother with the beloved disciple. The "other Mary," and another John, the Baptist, in whose name the chapel is consecrated, are in the side compartments. Above, in the smaller tracery, are the royal arms with the ancient motto " Dieu et mon droit," and the arms of the Prince Consort, with his device, one of the most touching in all heraldry, " Treu und Fest."

The window next to this, on the east, represents the scene of the Resurrection, and has this inscription painted on a tablet below— " The above window is presented to this Chapel Royal with Her Majesty's permission by Col. Wilson, gentleman harbinger in the reigns of King George IV., William IV., and her present Majesty Queen Victoria."

Facing it is one of a series of very pleasing

and harmoniously coloured designs, representing, above, the Transfiguration, and below, the Last Supper. Underneath are these words :—" In memory of Richard Lemon Lander, the discoverer of the source of the Niger, and the first Gold Medallist of the Royal Geographical Society. He was born at Truro in 1804, and died in the Island of Fernando Po in 1834, from wounds inflicted by the natives. This window is inserted, by her Majesty's permission, by some of his relations and friends, and by some of the Fellows of the Royal Geographical Society." The same series of designs is continued in the next window, in which we have, above, the Adoration of the Wise Men, and below, the Baptism. It is inscribed :—" To the Glory of God, in memory of Thomas Surr, who entered into rest December 23, 1860, aged 69; of Sarah Surr, who entered into rest October 8, 1868, aged 67 ; and of Timothy Surr, who entered into rest January 21, 1869, aged 75. They were buried in Norwood Cemetery. Dedicated by T. R. H., 1871."

On the opposite side, near the vestry door and the pulpit, is another window of similar design, but scarcely so brilliant as these two. The Ordination of Matthias is represented in the lower compartment, and the Day of Pentecost in the upper. It commemorates the late incumbent of the chapel :—"Ad sempiternam Dei gloriam et in memoriam Johannis Forster A.M. e Collegio Corporis Christi apud Cantabrigienses, rectoris ecclesiæ Divi Thomæ in agro Stamburniensi, qui olim sacerdotii munere annos xx. in hoc sacello pie sancteque perfunctus postremo mortem subitam occubuit die xxiv. mensis Julii anno sacro MDCCCLXVIII. ætatis suæ LIX. Hanc fenestram coloribus pingi voluit amicorum fides voluit munificentia hanc ædem frequentantium."

The next window is below the step of the chancel, and is larger than those above it. It contains figures of St. John, St. James, St. Andrew, St. Peter, St. Paul, and St. Philip, designed in a large style by Mr. Burne Jones. Underneath is this inscription, alluded to in a former chapter :—*

"In memory of Archibald Cameron, brother of Donald Cameron of Lochiel, who having been attainted after the Battle of Culloden in 1746, escaped to France, but returning to Scotland in 1753, was apprehended and executed. He was buried beneath the altar of this chapel. This window was inserted by her Majesty's permission, in place of a sculptured tablet which was erected by his grandson, Charles Hay

* See p. 214.

The Chapel as it is. Cameron, in 1846, and consumed by the fire which partially destroyed the chapel in 1864. (Christmas 1870.)"

Facing the Cameron window, on the western side of the chapel, is another of equal dimensions, and filled with what may safely be regarded as the finest glass in the church. The six lights are filled with representations of English royal saints, namely—above, St. Bertha, St. Edward, and St. Margaret (of Scotland), and below, St. Edmund, St. Etheldreda, and St. Oswald. It is pleasant to turn from the sad and humiliating memories connected with the Cameron memorial to this, our local expression of great national joy and thanksgiving. At the time of the memorable illness and recovery of his Royal Highness the Prince of Wales, many tokens of gratitude were manifested throughout the kingdom, and among all British subjects throughout the world. In the Savoy the tribute of thankfulness was rendered by the insertion of this painted window, executed by Messrs. Clayton and Bell. The inscription was most kindly and promptly contributed by the late Thomas Godfrey-Faussett, then Chapter Clerk of the Cathedral of Canterbury, and is as faultless in Latin verse, as it was fervent of national sentiment. Several accomplished scholars have most kindly favoured us with translations into

English verse. Our limits will only allow of the insertion of two.

✠ Quinto die mensis Martii. Anno Domini. 1872.
Mæstis ante hoc Altare nuper erat supplicare,
Clauderet ne vitam deinceps Walliæ dilectus Princeps.
Quo per morbum vix redacto, miro Dei benefacto
Vitream quam sic paramus, Deo grati consecramus.

This translation was kindly given by Mr. Godfrey-Faussett himself :—

> " Late before this altar kneeling,
> 　Sad we prayed with bated breath,
> That a much-loved Prince be spared us
> 　From the impending grasp of death.
> Thus when baffled was the sickness,—
> 　To God's wondrous grace be praise !—
> Storied glass in glad memorial
> 　Lo ! to Him we grateful raise."

This one is by the Rev. William Edward Heygate, M.A., Rector of Brightstone, Isle of Wight :—

> " We who before this Altar prayed
> 　That God our Prince would spare,
> To Him, Whose grace the fever stayed,
> 　This humble offering bear.
>
> May He who shone upon our night,
> 　As for our Prince we prayed,
> On us still pour a sacred light
> 　Whom He has thankful made."

APPENDIX A.

GRANT BY QUEEN ELEANOR TO HER SON EDMUND.

[*Great Cowcher*, II. 217, Duc. Lanc.]

ALIANORA, Dei gratia Regina Angliæ, domina Hiberniæ et ducissa Aquitanniæ, mater regis, universis præsentes literas visuris vel audituris salutem in Domino sempiternam. Noverit universitas vestra quod nos pro nobis et hæredibus nostris, dedimus, concessimus, et hac præsenti carta nostra confirmavimus Edmundo nato nostro carissimo, domos, gardinum, placeas et redditus cum pertinentiis suis quæ habuimus ex emptione nostra de præposito et capitulo domus Montis Jovis, et quæ quondam fuerunt carissimi avunculi nostri domini Petri Comitis Sabaudiæ, extra civitatem Londoniarum in parochia Sanctorum Innocentium de Albo Monasterio, habenda et tenenda prædicto Edmundo, hæredibus et assignatis suis, et quibuscumque vel cuicumque ea dare, vendere, legare vel quocunque modo assignare voluerit, libere, quiete, integre, bene et in pace, jure hæreditario, imperpetuum, absque ullo

retenemento vel reclamatione nostri vel hæredum
nostrorum. Et nos et hæredes nostri prædicto
Edmundo hæredibus et assignatis suis prædictis,
prædicta domos, gardinum, placeas et redditus cum
omnibus suis pertinentiis warantizabimus, acquie-
tabimus et contra omnes gentes defendemus
imperpetuum. In cujus rei testimonium præsenti
cartæ sigillum nostrum fecimus apponi. Hiis
testibus, dominis Guidone Feire, Roberto Pogeys,
Willelmo de Bluntesdone, Roberto de Mohon,
Ricardo Fokerande, Galfrido de Langele, militibus,
Dominis Willelmo de Percy, Hugone de Penna,
clericis et multis aliis. Datum apud Lotegarshall,
vicesimo quarto die Februarii, anno regni regis
Edwardi nati nostri duodecimo.

APPENDIX B.

The First Appointment of a Chancellor.

[Duchy of Lancaster Records, class xxv. A. 6.]

[MEMORANDUM quod de]cimo septimo die Aprilis
anno regni regis Edwardi tertii a conquestu Angliæ
quinquagesimo primo, apud Le [Savoye juxta] Westmonasterium, Johannes Rex Castellæ et Legionis,
dux Lancastriæ, in præsentia Roberti de Wylyngton
militis, Thomæ de Hongerforde, militis, et aliorum
de familia ipsius Regis ibidem præsentium, videlicet
in capella infra mansum dicti loci constructa, [con-
stituit] Thomam de Thelwall, clericum, cancellarium
suum infra ducatum et comitatum Lancastriæ, et

capto sacramento suo, idem Rex Magnum Sigillum suum pro regimine regalitatis comitatus palatini ibidem ordinatum manu sua propria prædicto Thomæ liberavit juxta officii sui debitum custodiendum.

APPENDIX C.

JOHN OF GAUNT, DUKE OF LANCASTER, TO HIS TREASURER : ALLOWANCE FOR WINE DESTROYED BY THE MOB.

[*Register*, xiii. f. 58 b.]

Pur.WILLIAM OVERBURY.

JOHAN par la grace de Dieu, roy de Castille et de Leon, duc de Lancastre, a nostre trescher et bien ame clerc, sire Johan de Norff', tresorer de nostre houstel, saluz. Nous vous mandons que en le procheine aconte quele nostre cher et bien ame esquier William Overbury nostre Butiller chargez en chief est a rendre devant vous, lui facez due allouance dun tonel de vyn de Gascoigne et un fatte de vyne Rynes par nous donez a nostre treschere cousine la contesse de Hereford, et mandez a Rocheford pur les esposailes de nostre tresame filz le conte de Derby. Item dune tonel de vyn de Gascoigne par nous dones a nostre treschere cousine la duchesse de Bretaigne en le moys de Decembre, un an passez. Item, dun tonel de vyn blank par nouz donez a mons. Thomas de Ildreton au chastel de Baumburgh. Item de

· deux tonelx de vyn de Gascoigne par nous donez a nostre treschere et bien amee dame Katerine de Swynford, lun envoiez de Bristuyt, et lautre envoie de nostre manoir de Rothewell. Item de deux tonelx de vin de Gascoigne par nous donez a nostre treschere et bien amee damoyselle Amye de Melburne lun envoiez de nostre chastel de Leycestre, et lautre envoie de nostre chastel de Tuttebury. Item dun tonel de vin de Gascoigne debrusez et perduz el carrage parentre Everwyk et nostre chastel de Pontefreſt, par un charieter de Tadecastre quele nous lui avons pardonez de nostre grace. Item dun tonel de vyn de Gascoigne debrusez et perduz en le carrage parentre nostre chastel de Knaresburgh et nostre chastel de Pontefreyt par William nostre charioter quele nous luy avons ensement pardonez de nostre grace. Item de xviij tonelx et un pipe et troys quarters dun pipe des diverses vynes destruz et perduz en nostre manoir de la Sauvoye par les communes rebelx en le temps del grant rumour. Item dun tonelle et un pipe et un quarter dun pipe de vyn destruz et perduz en nostre chastel de Hertford, meisme le temps et par meismes les communes rebelx. Item dune tonel de vyn de Gascoigne par nous donez a nostre treschere dame et soere le contesse de Beddeford. Et volons que cestes noz vous ent soient garrant sur vostre aconte. Done etc. a Londres, le xx jour de Feverer, lan etc. quint.*

* 5 Ric. II.

APPENDIX D.

EXPENSES OF THE GARDEN AT THE SAVOY.
[*Register*, xii. f. 151 b.]
Pur Sire W. de B. (WILLIAM DE BUGHBRIGG.)

JOHAN par la grace de Dieu etc. A noz bien amez clercs Sire Thomas de Mapelton et Sire Thomas de Neuton, auditours des comptes de noz ministres, et a lun de eux, saluz. Nous volons et vous mandons que en le prochein compte quelle nostre trescher clerc Sire William de B[ughbrigg] nostre receivour general est a rendre devant vous, ly allouez les sommes souescriptes, quelles il ad paiez diverses foitz de nostre commandement. Cest assavoir, xljs. et viijd. paiez pur cynk centz messes chauntez pur lalme de nostre trescher compaignon Mons. Wauter de Manny, un des chevaliers de la Garter; et xx.li. de nostre manoir de la Sauvoye envoiez de nostre commandement a Westm : le xx jour de Januer derrein passe. . . . . . . et xls. queux il ad paiez a nostre tresame clerc sire Johan de Yerdeburgh, clerc de nostre Garderobe, pur reparacion de nostre Gardein de la Sauvoye, l'an xlvj. Et cestes etc. Done etc. a la Sauvoye, le primer jour de May l'an xlvj. (Edward III.)

APPENDIX E.

Repairs of Houses at Savoy.
[*Ibid.* f. 153 b.]
Pur Johan de Shelton.

Johan, par la grace, etc. A nostre trescher clerc, Sire W. de B. nostre receivour general, saluz. Pource que noz maisons deinz nostre manoir de la Sauvoye, enbusoignent grandement de reparacion et amendement, et pour amender et reparailler noz ditz maisons, nous avons ordenez nostre ame servant Johan de Shelton pour noz deniers ent paiantz, et pur ly contrerouller des coustages myses et despenses queux il mettra en celle partie, avons assignez nostre bien ame clerc Sire Johan de Yerdeburgh, clerc de nostre garderobe ; voulons et vous mandons que les deniers queux par le contreroullement du dit Sire Johan vous purrez savoir le dit Johan Shelton avoir mys et despenduz entour lamendement et reparation de noz maisons susditz, ly paiez prestement de temps en temps des issues de vostre receyte, fesant endenteur parentre vous et ly de ce que ensi ly paierez, par la quelle et cestes noz lettres portans a voz comptes nous mandons as auditours dycelles que ils vous facent rebate, et due allouance en ycelles sanz contredit. Done, etc. a la Sauvoye, le derrier jour de Juyn, l'an etc. d'Engleterre xlvj, et de France xxxiij.

APPENDIX F.

WARRANT FOR REPAIR OF HOUSES
AND FENCING THE GARDEN IN THE SAVOY.

[*Ibid.* f. 154.]

Pur JOHAN SHELTON.

JOHAN, par la grace, etc. A nostre tresame clerc
Sire Johan de Yardeburgh, saluz. Pource que nous
avons ordenez et assignez nostre ame servant Johan
de Shelton affaire, amendre et reparailler noz
maisons deinz nostre manoir de la Sauvoye, a noz
coustages et despenses, et Nichol Gardiner, nostre
gardyner de noz gardeyns deinz nostre manoir, et
de achater pour noz deniers railles et verges neces-
saires et busoignables pur noz ditz gardyns quand
et a quelle temps que busoigne serra, et pur le grant
affiance que nous avons en vostre persone nous
vous avons assignez et assignons par ces presentes
nostre contreroullour de contrerouller sibien les
coustages quelles le dit Johan de Shelton mettra
entour l'amendement et reparacion de noz maisons
sus ditz, come les coustages et despenses queles le
dit Nichol ferra resonablement entour l'achate des
railles et verges busoignables pur le raillement de
noz gardeins sus ditz. Par quoy nous voulons et
vous mandons que les choses avant declarez vous
faces accomplier et perfourmer en et par la manere
quele mielz vous semblera affaire pur nostre honour
et profit, ses presentes a durer a nostre volunte.
Done, etc., a la Sauvoye, le derrier jour de Juyl,
l'an, etc., d'Engleterre xlvj, et de France xxxiij.

APPENDIX G.

[*Pat.* 1, *Henry IV.* m. 20.]

Charter declaring the possessions of the Duchy of Lancaster to be a separate inheritance, distinct from those of the Crown.

Recital that the King held the Duchy by inheritance, and of the charters of 28 Feb., 51 Edw. III. (1377); 16 Feb., 13 Ric. II. (1390); and 29 June, 20 Ric. II. (1396).

Declaration of the royal intention that the duchy and other estates of the heritage of Lancaster shall not be changed by the King's assumption of the royal dignity; the franchises held by John of Gaunt to be continued, and settled upon Henry IV. and his heirs; the estates to be governed by the like officers as before; the chancellor or treasurer of England not to intermeddle in presenting to church benefices; receivers, etc., to account before special auditors, not at the royal Exchequer. Westm., 14 Oct., 1 Henry IV.

APPENDIX H.

MORTMAIN LICENCE TO THE EXECUTORS OF
HENRY VII. TO FOUND A HOSPITAL AT THE
SAVOY.*

[*Pat.* 4, *Henry VIII.* pt. 1, m. 9.]

DE HOSPITALI DE SAVOY FUNDANDO.

Rex omnibus ad quos, etc., salutem. Cum nuper
per literas nostras patentes, sigillo nostro ducatus
nostri Lancastriæ sigillatas, quarum data est apud
London' tertio die Aprilis, anno regni nostri
secundo, dederimus, concesserimus et eadem carta
nostra confirmaverimus, Ricardo episcopo Wyn-
toniensi, custodi privati sigilli nostri; Ricardo
episcopo Londoniensi; Thomæ episcopo Dunolm-
ensi; Edmundo episcopo Sarisburiensi; Willelmo
episcopo Lincolniensi; Johanni episcopo Roffensi;
Thomæ comiti Arundell'; Thomæ comiti Surriæ,
thesaurario nostro Angliæ; Carolo Somerset,
militi, domino de Herbart, camerario nostro;
Johanni Fyneux, militi, capitali justiciario Banci
nostri; Roberto Rede, militi, capitali justiciario
communis Banci nostri; Magistro Johanni Yong,
custodi rotulorum cancellariæ nostræ; Thomæ
Lovell, militi, thesaurario Hospicii nostri; et
Johanni Cutte, sub-thesaurario nostro Angliæ,
executoribus testamenti Henrici nuper regis Angliæ

* This document has been printed by Rymer. *Fœdera*,
xiii. 333.

septimi, patris nostri illustrissimi, situm manerii de Savoye, sive quandam placeam sive peciam terræ vocatam *le Savoye*, nuper parcellam ducatus nostri prædicti, jacentem in parochiis Sancti Clementis Dacorum extra Barras Novi Templi London', et Beatæ Mariæ de Stronde in comitatu Middlesex', inter terram et mansionem episcopi Wygorniensis ex parte orientali, et terram episcopi Carliolensis, ex parte occidentali, et abuttantem super aquam Thamisiæ versus Austrum, et super viam nostram per quam itur de Stronde Crosse versus Charyng Crosse, versus Boriam.

Habendum et tenendum prædictum situm vocatum *le Savoy*, sive prædictam placeam seu peciam terræ vocatam *le Savoy* cum pertinentiis, præfatis executoribus, hæredibus, et assignatis suis imperpetuum de dono nostro quiete, de nobis et hæredibus nostris, absque compoto seu aliquo alio nobis, hæredibus, vel successoribus nostris pro eisdem reddendo, solvendo, vel faciendo, ad intentionem quod iidem executores, seu eorum aliqui sive aliquis quoddam hospitale in et super prædicto situ sive prædicta placea seu pecia terræ, vocata *le Savoy*, licentia nostra aut hæredum seu successorum nostrorum inde per ipsos seu eorum aliquos ad hoc optinenda, juxta ordinationem et statuta per ipsos seu eorum aliquos sive aliquem limitanda et ordinanda, erigere, fundare, creare, et stabilire possent seu posset, aut erigi, creari, fundari, et stabiiri facerent seu faceret, prout in eisdem literis nostris patentibus inter alia plenius apparet. Sciatis quod nos, de gratia nostra speciali, ac de certa scientia et mero motu nostris, prædictas literas nostras patentes, ac donum et concessionem prædicta, necnon omnia et singula in eisdem literis nostris patentibus contenta et specificata, rata habentes et grata, ea per præsentes ratificamus, approbamus et confirmamus. Et insuper, de uberiori gratia nostra, ac ex scientia et mero motu nostris prædictis, concessimus et licentiam dedimus ac per præsentes licentiam damus et concedimus, pro nobis et hæredibus nostris, quantum in nobis est, præfatis executoribus, quod ipsi seu eorum aliqui superviventes, seu eorum aliquis supervivens, quoddam hospitale perpetuum de quinque capellanis perpetuis secularibus, videlicet, de uno magistro et quatuor aliis capellanis, infra et super situm prædictum sive prædictam placeam seu peciam terræ vocatam *le Savoy*, ad laudem et honorem domini nostri Jesu Christi, Beatissimæque semper Virginis Mariæ, Matris ejus, ac Sancti Johannis Baptistæ, ad exorandum pro bono statu nostro et Katerinæ consortis nostræ dum vixerimus, et pro animabus nostris cum ab hac luce migraverimus, et specialissime pro salute animarum prædicti nuper regis patris nostri, et Elizabethæ nuper consortis suæ, matris nostræ præcarissimæ, necnon Arthuri, primogeniti eorum nuper Principis Walliæ, ducis Cornubiæ et comitis Cestriæ, fratris nostri, juxta ordinationes et statuta eorundem executorum, sive eorum aliquorum, seu eorum alicujus, fundatoris sive fundatorum ejusdem hospitalis fienda et limitanda, fundare, erigere, creare, facere et stabilire possint et possit. Et quod hospitale prædictum, cum sic fundatum, erectum et stabilitum existat, *Hospitale Henrici nuper Regis Angliæ Septimi de Savoy*, nominetur, vocetur, et appelletur. Quodque magister Hospitalis illius et successores sui magistri ejusdem Hospitalis et capellani hospitalis illius, *Magister et capellani Hospitalis Henrici nuper Regis Angliæ Septimi de Savoy*, similiter nominentur, vocentur et appellentur.

Et quod iidem Magister et capellani, sint incorporati et uniti, et sint unum corpus in re et in nomine, habeantque successionem perpetuam.

Et quod iidem Magister et capellani, et eorum successores, per idem nomen et sub eodem nomine, sint personæ habiles et capaces in lege ad perquirendum et recipiendum terras, tenementa, annuitates, redditus, servicia, advocationes ecclesiarum, prioratuum, emolumenta, possessiones, et hæreditamenta quæcumque, necnon bona et catalla tam de dono nostro quam de quibuscumque personis, ea eis dare, legare, seu assignare volentibus, sibi et successoribus suis imperpetuum.

Et quod iidem Magister et capellani, et eorum successores, habeant unum sigillum commune pro negotiis Hospitalis prædicti agendis.

Et quod iidem Magister et capellani et eorum successores, magistri et capellani Hospitalis prædicti, per nomen *Magistri et capellanorum*

Hospitalis Henrici nuper regis Angliæ Septimi de Savoy, implacitare et implacitari, prosequi et defendi possint in omnibus et singulis causis, querelis, actionibus realibus, personalibus et mixtis, cujuscunque fuerint generis sive naturæ, ac respondere et responderi, defendere et defendi valeant, sub nomine prædicto in eisdem in quibuscumque curiis et locis, coram quibuscumque justiciariis et judicibus tam spiritualibus quam temporalibus.

Et ulterius, de uberiori gratia nostra concedimus et licentiam damus pro nobis et hæredibus nostris, per præsentes, quod, postquam Hospitale prædictum, ut prædicitur, fundatum, erectum, creatum et stabilitum fuerit, prædicti executores et eorum quilibet, ac aliæ quæcumque personæ et quæcumque alia persona, terras, tenementa, redditus, servicia, reversiones, advocationes ecclesiarum, prioratuum, hospitalia, liberas capellas, ac alia beneficia ecclesiastica quæcumque, necnon omnia et omnimoda alia hæreditamenta et possessiones quascumque ad valorem quingentarum marcarum per annum, ultra omnia onera et reprisas, tam de feodo suo proprio quam alieno, licet de nobis in capite vel aliter vel aliquo alio modo seu de aliquibus aliis personis sive de aliqua alia persona quacumque teneantur, Magistro et capellanis Hospitalis prædicti pro tempore existentibus et successoribus suis, dare concedere, appropriare, consolidare, annectere, unire et assignare possint et possit; et eisdem Magistro et capellanis, et successoribus suis, quod ipsi terras et tenementa, redditus, reversiones, servicia, advocationes ecclesiarum, prioratuum, hospitalia, liberas capellas, ac alia beneficia ecclesiastica quæcumque, necnon omnia et omnimoda alia hæreditamenta et possessiones quascumque, ad annuum valorem prædictum ultra omnia onera et reprisas, a præfatis executoribus, seu eorum aliquibus sive aliquo aut quibuscumque aliis personis, seu quacumque alia persona, ea eis dare, legare, appropriare, concedere, consolidare, annectere, unire et assignare volentibus sive volenti, recipere possint et tenere sibi et successoribus suis imperpetuum. Tenore præsentium similiter licentiam damus specialem ad sustentationem suam et ad quædam alia misericordiæ et pietatis opera et onera, in fundatione et ordinatione Hospitalis prædicti, per prædictos executores, seu eorum aliquos vel aliquem, limitanda et assignanda, facienda et perimplenda; statuto de terris seu tenementis ad manum mortuam non ponendis edito, non obstante; et absque impetitione, impedimento, seu perturbatione nostri aut hæredum sive successorum nostrorum seu aliorum quorumcumque, et absque aliqua inquisitione, sive aliquibus inquisitionibus, virtute alicujus brevis sive mandati nostri, seu aliquorum brevium mandatorum nostrorum hæredum et successorum nostrorum de *ad quod dampnum*, seu alicujus alterius brevis sive mandati nostri, in ea

Appendix. parte capiendi seu prosequendi, et absque aliqua alia licentia nostra, seu aliis literis patentibus eis in hac parte concedendis vel fiendis ; dicto statuto de terris et tenementis ad manum mortuam non ponendis, aut aliquo alio statuto, actu, ordinatione, seu restrictione in contrarium factis, editis, sive ordinatis, aut aliqua alia re, causa vel materia quacumque, in aliquo non obstante. Eo quod expressa mentio de vero valore annuo, aut certitudine præmissorum in præsentibus minime facta existit, aut aliquo statuto, actu, ordinatione, sive restrictione, aut aliqua alia causa, re vel materia quacumque, in aliquo non obstante. In cujus etc.

Teste Rege, apud Westmonasterium, Quinto die Julii.

Per breve de privato sigillo et de data etc.

INDEX.

·*Printed by* R. & R. CLARK, *Edinburgh.*